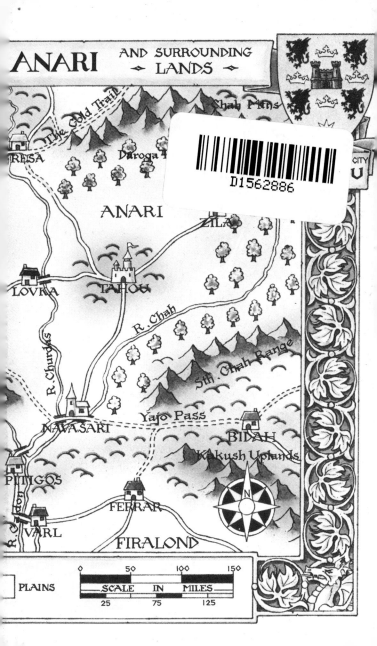

ANARI AND SURROUNDING ~ LANDS ~

Shah Mtns

The Gold Trail

RESA

Daroga

CITY

U

ANARI

ZILA

LOVKA

TAHOU

R. Chah

R. Churkas

Sth. Chah Range

Yajo Pass

NAVASARI

BIDAH

Kakush Uplands

PITIGOS

FERRAR

VARL

FIRALOND

PLAINS

0   50   100   150
SCALE   IN   MILES
25   75   125

The bearer of this scroll, namely,

is a master in the
Order of the Kai

While on your quest, word has reached you that Sommerlund has suffered a great defeat at the city of Ruanon, but morale among your people remains high. Boldly, your homeland continues its valiant fight against the evil forces of the Darklords.

The messenger who has delivered this news also informs you that the King himself has ordered a Skyship placed in your command and has awarded you the rank of Warmarshall of the Royal Estates. You proudly accept the use of the Skyship as well as the two platinum badges that signify your new rank. You are now the youngest general in the Sommerlund army.

But once again you must continue with your quest. You are the last hope for the rebirth of the Kai! Ahead lies the greatest danger you have ever faced ...

JOE DEVER, author of the Lone Wolf and World of Lone Wolf series, is a contributing editor to the White Dwarf, Britain's leading fantasy games magazine. **LONE WOLF** is the culmination of seven years of developing the world of the Magnamund. He is also the author of the huge compendium based on the world of the Magnamund, *The Magnamund Companion*.

BOOK 9

The Cauldron of Fear

Joe Dever

Illustrated by Brian Williams

 BOOKS FOR YOUNG ADULTS

B

BERKLEY BOOKS, NEW YORK

This Berkley / Pacer book contains the complete
text of the original edition.

THE CAULDRON OF FEAR

A Berkley/Pacer Book, published by arrangement
with Century Hutchinson Ltd.

PRINTING HISTORY
Beaver Books edition published 1987
Berkley/Pacer edition / May 1988

All rights reserved.
Text copyright © 1987 by Joe Dever.
Illustrations copyright © 1987 by Century Hutchinson Ltd.
This book may not be reproduced in whole or in part,
by mimeograph or any other means, without permission.
For information address: Arrow Books Limited,
62-65 Chandos Place, London WC2N 4NW.

ISBN: 0-425-10848-1
RL: 9.5

Pacer is a trademark belonging to
The Putnam Publishing Group.

A BERKLEY BOOK ® TM 757,375
Berkley/Pacer Books are published by
The Berkley Publishing Group,
200 Madison Avenue, New York, NY 10016.
The name "BERKLEY" and the "B" logo
are trademarks belonging to Berkley Publishing Corporation.

PRINTED IN THE UNITED STATES OF AMERICA

10   9   8   7   6

To Spencer and Louise

ACTION CHART

MAGNAKAI DISCIPLINES   NOTES

1	
2	
3	
4	4th Magnakai discipline if you have completed 1 Magnakai adventure successfully
5	5th Magnakai discipline if you have completed 2 Magnakai adventures successfully
6	6th Magnakai discipline if you have completed 3 Magnakai adventures successfully

MAGNAKAI LORE - CIRCLE   BONUSES

	CS	EP		CS	EP
CIRCLE OF FIRE	+1	+2	CIRCLE OF SOLARIS	+1	+3
CIRCLE OF LIGHT	0	+3	CIRCLE OF THE SPIRIT	+3	+3

BACKPACK (max. 8 articles)	MEALS
1	
2	
3	— 3 EP if no Meal available when instructed to eat.
4	BELT POUCH Containing Gold Crowns (50 maximum)
5	
6	
7	
8 Can be discarded when not in combat.	

CS = COMBAT SKILL   EP = ENDURANCE POINTS

COMBAT SKILL	ENDURANCE POINTS
	Can never go above initial score 0 = dead

COMBAT RECORD

ENDURANCE POINTS		ENDURANCE POINTS
LONE WOLF	COMBAT RATIO	ENEMY
LONE WOLF	COMBAT RATIO	ENEMY
LONE WOLF	COMBAT RATIO	ENEMY
LONE WOLF	COMBAT RATIO	ENEMY
LONE WOLF	COMBAT RATIO	ENEMY

MAGNAKAI RANK

SPECIAL ITEMS LIST

DESCRIPTION	KNOWN EFFECTS

WEAPONS LIST

WEAPONS (maximum 2 Weapons)

1	
2	

If holding Weapon and appropriate Weaponmastery in combat +3 CS. If combat entered carrying no Weapon −4CS.

WEAPONMASTERY CHECKLIST

DAGGER		SPEAR	
MACE		SHORT SWORD	
WARHAMMER		BOW	
AXE		SWORD	
QUARTERSTAFF		BROADSWORD	

QUIVER & ARROWS

Quiver	No. of arrows carried
YES/NO	

THE STORY SO FAR

You are the warrior, Lone Wolf, last of the Kai Masters of Sommerlund and sole survivor of the massacre that destroyed your kinsmen during a bitter war with your age-old enemies – the Darklords of Helgedad.

Many centuries have passed since Sun Eagle, the first of your kind, established the Order of the Kai. Aided by the magicians of Dessi, he completed a perilous quest to find seven crystals of power, known as the Lorestones of Nyxator, and upon their discovery he unlocked a wisdom and strength that lay within both the Lorestones and himself. He recorded the nature of his discoveries and his experiences in a great tome entitled *The Book of the Magnakai*. You have discovered this lost Kai treasure and have given a solemn pledge to restore the Kai to their former glory, thereby ensuring the security of your land in the years to come. However, your diligent study of this ancient book has enabled you to master only three of the ten Magnakai Disciplines. To fulfil your pledge, you must complete the quest first undertaken by Sun Eagle over one thousand years ago. By doing so successfully, you, too, will acquire the power and wisdom of the Magnakai, which is held within the Lorestones' crystal forms.

11

Already your quest has taken you far from your northern homeland. Following in the footsteps of the first Kai Grand Master, you journeyed to Dessi and sought the help of the Elder Magi, the magicians that aided Sun Eagle on his quest long ago. There you learned that one of the seven Lorestones was still present in their land, hidden deep inside an island stronghold known as Kazan-Oud, or Castle Death. You survived the perils of Castle Death and emerged triumphant, having achieved what the Elder Magi had believed to be impossible. During the victory celebrations held in your honour, you learned that for centuries the Elder Magi had been expecting your coming. An ancient Dessi legend tells of the birth and rise to greatness of two 'koura-tas-kai', which means 'sons of the sun'. One was named 'Ikar', which means 'eagle', and the other was named 'Skarn', which means 'wolf'. A prophecy foretold that the koura-tas-kai would each come from the north to seek the council of the Elder Magi in order that they might fulfil a great quest. Although separated by several centuries, they would share one spirit, one purpose and one destiny — to triumph over the champions of darkness in an age of great peril. Your victory at Kazan-Oud proved that you were Skarn — the wolf of Dessi legend — and in keeping with their ancient vows the Elder Magi promised to help you complete the Magnakai quest.

In Elzian, the capital of Dessi, you were tutored in the histories of Magnamund and received lessons in lore that you would have learned from Kai Masters if only they, like you, had survived the murderous Darklord attack on the Kai monastery eleven years ago. You were eager to learn all that your tutor, Lord Rimoah, could teach you in preparation for the next stage of your quest, but grim news from the Darklands cut short your tuition. In the Darklord city of Helgedad a civil war had erupted, following your defeat of Haakon, Archlord of the Black City. After five years, the battle for the throne of Helgedad had finally been won by a Darklord called Gnaag. The other Darklords, now united behind this new leader, were ordered to amass huge armies in preparation for the conquest of Magnamund. So swiftly did their Giak legions grow in numbers that the Elder Magi ceased their counselling and arranged for you to begin at once the search for the third Lorestone. Guided by Lord Paido, a warrior-magician of Dessi, you set off on a perilous journey across the freelands of Talestria on your way to the jungle-swamps of the Danarg. There, in an ancient temple that was once the Elder Magi's most sacred place of worship, you succeeded in discovering the object of your quest. However, during your escape from the Danarg, your guide, Lord Paido, was captured by Darklord agents, and upon your return to Elzian you learned the fearful news that the Darklords were now waging open war throughout Magnamund. Several lands, after brief but futile resistance, had been overrun completely by Darklord armies, others had surrendered without fighting in the face of their determined might, and sadly there were others who chose to betray former friends and allies by joining the Darklord cause, in the misguided hope that they would share in the spoils of victory, following the triumph of Darklord Gnaag. One such land was Vassagonia, a powerful desert realm to the north of Dessi. Already her armies had invaded the neighbouring territories of Casiorn and Cloeasia, and were preparing to march

13

through the Republic of Anari in order to join Gnaag's horde now advancing across the plain of Slovia. The thought of such an eventuality filled the Elder Magi with dread, for the Lorestone you must find next lies deep below the streets of Tahou, the capital of Anari, in an ancient city built during the dawn of Magnamund. If Tahou were to fall before your arrival the chances of your completing your quest successfully would be slim indeed, even for a warrior of your renowned skill and daring.

Whilst preparations were being made for your journey you learned that the Darklords had attacked and captured Ruanon, the southernmost province of your homeland of Sommerlund. The news of this calamity shook your resolve and filled you with the desire to forego the journey to Tahou and return home without delay. The Elder Magi implored you not to abandon your quest and you faced a difficult and crucial decision. Which should you honour: your vow to complete the Magnakai quest or your oath of loyalty to your King, an oath which pledged your service in the defence of the sun-realm? Fortunately, the surprise arrival of an old friend was to decide the matter for you. Magemaster Banedon, envoy of the Brotherhood of the Crystal Star – the magician's guild of Sommerlund – landed unexpectedly at Elzian aboard his flying ship *Skyrider*. He and his dwarven crew were warmly greeted, for Banedon, a frequent and favoured visitor to Dessi, was highly respected by the Elder Magi for his mastery of new magic. Six years had passed since last you met and there was much you wished to discuss and reminisce about, but there was an urgent matter of duty to perform first. Banedon had been sent by King

Ulnar of Sommerlund to deliver into your hand a royal missive concerning your quest. The scroll, written and sealed by the King himself, ordered you to pursue the Magnakai quest above all other duties. It ended with the words: 'Sommerlund has suffered a grievous defeat at Ruanon, but the will of the people is undaunted and the strength of our army undiminished. Boldly we will resist our enemies so long as there is hope of the rebirth of the Kai.'

Banedon informed you that the King had ordered that he and his skyship be placed under your command. He also delivered the news that the King had bestowed upon you the rank of Warmarshall of the Royal Estates. Proudly you accepted from Banedon two platinum badges, each crafted in the shape of a blazing sun, and affixed them to the collar of your Kai tunic. They signified that you were now a general of the Sommlending army, the youngest general there had ever been. The honour bestowed upon you lifted your spirits, and the news that Banedon would be joining your quest helped greatly to allay your fear of the dangers that lay ahead. For two years Banedon had lived in Tahou as Journeymaster to his guild; his knowledge of the city and of the Tahou Cauldron, the entrance to the ancient metropolis, which lies buried deep beneath the city streets, would be especially useful.

On the eve of your journey to Tahou, the Elder Magi convened a meeting of the High Council. A golden torch was lit and placed in the centre of their great cylindrical council chamber as a symbol of their hopes and prayers for your success.

'This torch shall burn so long as you, Lone Wolf, pursue your destiny along the path of the Magnakai,' said Lord Rimoah, speaker for the High Council. Before the gathering of Elders you reaffirmed your vow to restore the Kai and, as if kindled by a sudden gust of wind, the torch flared brightly, bathing the chamber in its vivid golden glow. As one, the Elders rose from their seats and intoned their blessing: 'May the gods Ishir and Kai protect you on your journey into darkness, Kor-Skarn.'

THE GAME RULES

You keep a record of your adventure on the *Action Chart* that you will find in the front of this book. For further adventuring you can copy out the chart yourself or get it photocopied.

During your training as a Kai Master you have developed fighting prowess – COMBAT SKILL – and physical stamina – ENDURANCE. Before you set off on your adventure you need to measure how effective your training has been. To do this take a pencil and, with your eyes closed, point with the blunt end of it on to the *Random Number Table* on the last page of this book. If you pick *0* it counts as zero.

The first number that you pick from the *Random Number Table* in this way represents your COMBAT SKILL. Add 10 to the number you picked and write the total in the COMBAT SKILL section of your *Action Chart*. (ie, if your pencil fell on the number 4 in the *Random Number Table* you would write in a COMBAT SKILL of 14). When you fight, your COMBAT SKILL will be pitted against that of your enemy. A high score in this section is therefore very desirable.

The second number that you pick from the *Random Number Table* represents your powers of ENDURANCE. Add 20 to this number and write the total in the ENDURANCE section of your *Action Chart* (ie, if your pencil fell on the number 6 on the *Random Number Table* you would have 26 ENDURANCE points).

If you are wounded in combat you will lose ENDURANCE points. If at any time your ENDURANCE points fall to zero, you are dead and the adventure is over. Lost ENDURANCE points can be regained during the course of the adventure, but your number of ENDURANCE points can never rise above the number you started with.

If you have successfully completed any of the previous adventures in the Lone Wolf series, you you can carry your current scores of COMBAT SKILL and ENDURANCE points over to Book 9. You may also carry over any Weapons and Special Items you have in your possession at the end of your last adventure, and these should be entered on your new *Action Chart* (you are still limited to two Weapons and eight Backpack Items).

You may choose one bonus Magnakai Discipline to add to your *Action Chart* for every Lone Wolf Magnakai adventure you complete successfully (books 6–12).

MAGNAKAI DISCIPLINES

During your training as a Kai Lord, and in the course of the adventures that led to the discovery of *The Book of the Magnakai*, you have mastered all ten of the basic warrior skills known as the Kai Disciplines.

After studying *The Book of the Magnakai*, you have also reached the rank of Kai Master Superior, which means that you have learnt *three* of the Magnakai Disciplines listed below. It is up to you to choose which three skills these are. As all of the Magnakai Disciplines will be of use to you at some point on your adventure, pick your three with care. The correct use of a Magnakai Discipline at the right time can save your life.

The Magnakai skills are divided into groups, each of which is governed by a separate school of training. These groups are called 'Lore-circles'. By mastering all the Magnakai Disciplines in a particular Lore-circle, you can gain an increase in your COMBAT SKILL and ENDURANCE points score. (See the section 'Lore-circles of the Magnakai' for details of these bonuses.)

When you have chosen your three Magnakai Disciplines, enter them in the Magnakai Disciplines section of your *Action Chart*.

Weaponmastery

This Magnakai Discipline enables a Kai Master to become proficient in the use of all types of weapon. When you enter combat with a weapon you have mastered, you add 3 points to your COMBAT SKILL. The rank of Kai Master Superior, with which you begin the Magnakai series, means you are skilled in *three* of the weapons listed overleaf.

SPEAR

DAGGER

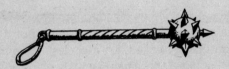

MACE

SHORT SWORD

WARHAMMER

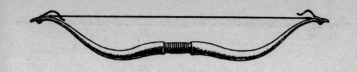

BOW

QUARTERSTAFF

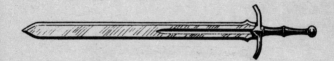

BROADSWORD

AXE

SWORD

If you choose this skill, write 'Weaponmastery: +3 COMBAT SKILL points' on your *Action Chart*, and tick your chosen weapons on the weapons list that appears on page 9. You cannot carry more than two weapons.

Animal Control

This Magnakai Discipline enables a Kai Master to communicate with most animals and to determine their purpose and intentions. It also enables a Kai Master to fight from the saddle with great advantage.

If you choose this skill, write 'Animal Control' on your *Action Chart*.

Curing

The possessor of this skill can restore 1 lost ENDURANCE point to his total for every numbered section of the book through which he passes, provided he is not involved in combat. (This can only be done after his ENDURANCE has fallen below its original level.) This Magnakai Discipline also enables a Kai Master to cure disease, blindness and any combat wounds sustained by others, as well as himself. Using the knowledge mastery of this skill provides will also allow a Kai Master to identify the properties of any herbs, roots and potions that may be encountered during the adventure.

If you choose this skill, write 'Curing: +1 ENDURANCE point for each section without combat' on your *Action Chart*.

22

Invisibility

This Magnakai skill allows a Kai Master to blend in with his surroundings, even in the most exposed terrain. It will enable him to mask his body heat and scent, and to adopt the dialect and mannerisms of any town or city that he visits.

If you choose this skill, write 'Invisibility' on your *Action Chart*.

Huntmastery

This skill ensures that a Kai Master will never starve in the wild; he will always be able to hunt for food, even in areas of wasteland and desert. It also enables a Kai Master to move with great speed and dexterity and will allow him to ignore any extra loss of COMBAT SKILL points due to a surprise attack or ambush.

If you choose this skill, write 'Huntmastery' on your *Action Chart*.

Pathsmanship

In addition to the basic skill of being able to recognize the correct path in unknown territory, the Magnakai skill of Pathsmanship will enable a Kai Master to read foreign languages, decipher symbols, read footprints and tracks (even if they have been disturbed), and detect the presence of most traps. It also grants him the gift of always knowing intuitively the position of north.

If you choose this skill, write 'Pathsmanship' on your *Action Chart*.

Psi-surge

This psychic skill enables a Kai Master to attack an enemy using the force of his mind. It can be used as well as normal combat weapons and adds 4 extra points to your COMBAT SKILL.

It is a powerful Discipline, but it is also a costly one. For every round of combat in which you use Psi-surge, you must deduct 2 ENDURANCE points. A weaker form of Psi-surge called Mindblast can be used against an enemy without losing any ENDURANCE points, but it will add only 2 extra points to your COMBAT SKILL. Psi-surge cannot be used if your ENDURANCE falls to 6 points or below, and not all of the creatures encountered on your adventure will be affected by it; you will be told if a creature is immune.

If you choose this skill, write 'Psi-surge +4 COMBAT SKILL points but −2 ENDURANCE points per round' or 'Mindblast: +2 COMBAT SKILL points' on your *Action Chart.*

Psi-screen

Many of the hostile creatures that inhabit Magnamund have the ability to attack you using their Mindforce. The Magnakai Discipline of Psi-screen prevents you from losing any ENDURANCE points when subjected to this form of attack and greatly increases your defence against supernatural illusions and hypnosis.

If you choose this skill, write 'Psi-screen: no points lost when attacked by Mindforce' on your *Action Chart.*

24

Nexus

Mastery of this Magnakai skill will enable you to withstand extremes of heat and cold without losing ENDURANCE points, and to move items by your powers of concentration alone.

If you choose this skill, write 'Nexus' on your *Action Chart*.

Divination

This skill may warn a Kai Master of imminent or unseen danger, or enable him to detect an invisible or hidden enemy. It may also reveal the true purpose or intent of a stranger or strange object encountered in your adventure. Divination may enable you to communicate telepathically with another person and to sense if a creature possesses psychic abilities.

If you choose this skill, write 'Divination' on your *Action Chart*.

If you successfully complete the mission as set in Book 9 of the Lone Wolf Magnakai series, you may add a further Magnakai Discipline of your choice to your *Action Chart* in Book 10. This additional skill, together with your other Magnakai skills and any Special Items that you have found and been able to keep during your adventures, may then be used in the next adventure, which is called *The Dungeons of Torgar*.

EQUIPMENT

Before leaving Dessi on your journey to the city of Tahou, the Elder Magi give you a map of the Republic of Anari and its surrounding lands (see the inside front cover of this book), and a pouch of gold. To find out how much gold is in the pouch, pick a number from the *Random Number Table*. Add 10 to the number you have picked. The total equals the number of Gold Crowns inside the pouch, and you should now enter this number in the 'Gold Crowns' section of your *Action Chart*. If you have successfully completed books *1–8* of the Lone Wolf adventures, you may add this sum to the total sum of Crowns you already possess. You can carry a maximum of only fifty Crowns, but additional Crowns can be left in safe-keeping at your Kai monastery.

The Elder Magi offer you a choice of equipment to aid you on your perilous mission. You can take five items from the list below, again adding to these, if necessary, any you may already possess. However, remember that you can carry a maximum of two Weapons and eight Backpack Items.

SWORD (Weapons)

BOW (Weapons)

QUIVER (Special Items) This contains six arrows. Tick them off as they are used.

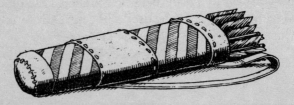

26

ROPE (Backpack Items)

POTION OF LAUMSPUR (Backpack Items) This potion restores 4 ENDURANCE points to your total when swallowed after combat. There is enough for only one dose.

LANTERN (Backpack Items)
MACE (Weapons)

3 MEALS (Meals) Each Meal takes up one space in your Backpack.

DAGGER (Weapons)

3 FIRESEEDS (Special Items) When thrown against a hard surface, these Fireseeds explode and burn fiercely.

List the five items that you choose on your *Action Chart*, under the heading given in brackets, and make a note of any effect they may have on your ENDURANCE points or COMBAT SKILL.

How to carry equipment

Now that you have your equipment, the following list shows you how it is carried. You do not need to make notes but you can refer back to this list in the course of your adventure.

SWORD – carried in the hand.
BOW – carried in the hand.
QUIVER – slung over your shoulder.
ROPE – carried in the Backpack.
POTION OF LAUMSPUR – carried in the Backpack.
LANTERN – carried in the Backpack.
MACE – carried in the hand.
MEALS – carried in the Backpack.
DAGGER – carried in the hand.
FIRESEEDS – carried in your pocket.

How much can you carry?

Weapons
The maximum number of weapons that you may carry is *two*.

Backpack Items
These must be stored in your Backpack. Because space is limited, you may keep a maximum of only eight articles, including Meals, in your Backpack at any one time.

Special Items
Special Items are not carried in the Backpack. When you discover a Special Item, you will be told how to carry it.

The maximum number of Special Items that can be carried on any adventure is twelve. Surplus Special Items may be left for safe-keeping at your Kai monastery.

Gold Crowns
These are always carried in the Belt Pouch. It will hold a maximum of fifty Crowns.

Food
Food is carried in your Backpack. Each Meal counts as one item.

Any item that may be of use and can be picked up on your adventure and entered on your *Action Chart* is given initial capitals (eg Gold Dagger, Magic Pendant) in the text. Unless you are told it is a Special Item, carry it in your Backpack.

How to use your equipment

Weapons

Weapons aid you in combat. If you have the Magnakai Discipline of Weaponmastery and a correct weapon, it adds 3 points to your COMBAT SKILL. If you enter a combat with no weapons, deduct 4 points from your COMBAT SKILL and fight with your bare hands. If you find a weapon during the adventure, you may pick it up and use it. (Remember that you can only carry *two* weapons at once.)

Bow and Arrows

During your adventure there will be opportunities to use a bow and arrow. If you equip yourself with this weapon, and you possess at least one arrow, you may use it when the text of a particular section allows you to do so. The bow is a useful weapon, for it enables you to hit an enemy at a distance. However, a bow cannot be used in hand-to-hand combat, therefore it is strongly recommended that you also equip yourself with a close combat weapon, such as a sword or mace.

In order to use a bow you must possess a quiver and at least one arrow. Each time the bow is used, erase an arrow from your *Action Chart*. A bow cannot, of course, be used if you exhaust your supply of arrows, but the opportunity may arise during your adventure for you to replenish your stock of arrows.

If you have the Magnakai Discipline of Weaponmastery with a bow, you may add 3 to any number that you choose from the *Random Number Table*, when using the bow. If you enter combat armed only with a bow, you must deduct 4 points from your COMBAT SKILL and fight with your bare hands.

Backpack Items

During your travels you will discover various useful items which you may wish to keep. (Remember you can only carry a maximum of eight items in your Backpack at any time.) You may exchange or discard them at any point when you are not involved in combat.

Special Items

Special Items are not carried in the Backpack. When you discover a Special Item, you will be told how to carry it. If you have successfully completed previous Lone Wolf books, you may already possess Special Items.

The maximum number of Special Items that a Kai Master can carry during an adventure is twelve. Surplus Special Items may be left in safe keeping at your Kai monastery.

Gold Crowns

The currency of Anari is the Lune, but Gold Crowns are readily accepted at an exchange rate of 4 Lune for every 1 Gold Crown.

Food

You will need to eat regularly during your adventure. If you do not have any food when you are instructed to eat a Meal, you will lose 3 ENDURANCE points. If you have chosen the Magnakai Discipline of Huntmastery as one of your skills, you will not need to tick off a Meal when instructed to eat.

31

Potion of Laumspur
This is a healing potion that can restore 4 ENDURANCE points to your total when swallowed after combat. There is enough for one dose only. If you discover any other potion during the adventure, you will be informed of its effect. All potions are Backpack Items.

RULES FOR COMBAT

There will be occasions during your adventure when you have to fight an enemy. The enemy's COMBAT SKILL and ENDURANCE points are given in the text. Lone Wolf's aim in the combat is to kill the enemy by reducing his ENDURANCE points to zero while losing as few ENDURANCE points as possible himself.

At the start of a combat, enter Lone Wolf's and the enemy's ENDURANCE points in the appropriate boxes on the Combat Record section of your *Action Chart*.

The sequence for combat is as follows:

1. Add any extra points gained through your Magnakai Disciplines and Special Items to your current COMBAT SKILL total.

2. Subtract the COMBAT SKILL of your enemy from this total. The result is your *Combat Ratio*. Enter it on the *Action Chart*.

Example

Lone Wolf (COMBAT SKILL 15) is attacked by a Nightstalker (COMBAT SKILL 22). He is not given the opportunity to evade combat, but must stand and fight as the creature leaps on him. Lone Wolf has the Magnakai Discipline of Psi-surge to which the Nightstalker is not immune, so Lone Wolf adds 4 points to his COMBAT SKILL giving him a total COMBAT SKILL of 19.

He subtracts the Nightstalker's COMBAT SKILL from his own, giving a *Combat Ratio* of −3. (19 − 22 = −3). −3 is noted on the *Action Chart* as the *Combat Ratio*.

3. When you have your *Combat Ratio*, pick a number from the *Random Number Table*.

4. Turn to the *Combat Results Table* on the inside back cover of the book. Along the top of the chart are shown the *Combat Ratio* numbers. Find the number that is the same as your *Combat Ratio* and cross-reference it with the random number that you have picked (the random numbers appear on the side of the chart). You now have the number of ENDURANCE points lost by both Lone Wolf and his enemy in this round of combat. (*E* represents points lost by the enemy; *LW* represents points lost by Lone Wolf.)

Example

The *Combat Ratio* between Lone Wolf and the Nightstalker has been established as −3. If the number taken from the *Random Number Table* is a 6, then the result of the first round of combat is:

Lone Wolf loses 3 ENDURANCE points (plus an additional 2 points for using Psi-surge)
Nightstalker loses 6 ENDURANCE points.

5. On the *Action Chart*, mark the changes in ENDURANCE points to the participants in the combat.

6. Unless otherwise instructed, or unless you have an option to evade, the next round of combat now starts.

7. Repeat the sequence from Stage 3.

This process of combat continues until ENDURANCE points of either the enemy or Lone Wolf are reduced to zero, at which point the one with the zero score is declared dead. If Lone Wolf is dead, the adventure is over. If the enemy is dead, Lone Wolf proceeds but with his ENDURANCE points reduced.

A summary of Combat Rules appears on the page after the *Random Number Table*.

Evasion of combat

During your adventure you may be given the chance to evade combat. If you have already engaged in a round of combat and decide to evade, calculate the combat for that round in the usual manner. All points lost by the enemy as a result of that round are ignored, and you make your escape. Only Lone Wolf may lose ENDURANCE points during that round, but then that is the risk of running away! You may only evade if the text of the particular section allows you to do so.

LEVELS OF MAGNAKAI TRAINING

The following table is a guide to the rank and titles that are achieved by Kai Masters at each stage of their training. As you successfully complete each adventure in the Lone Wolf Magnakai series, you will gain an additional Magnakai Discipline and progress towards the ultimate distinction of a Kai Warrior – Kai Grand Mastership.

No. of Magnakai Disciplines mastered by Kai Master	Magnakai Rank
1	Kai Master
2	Kai Master Senior
3	Kai Master Superior – *You begin the Lone Wolf Magnakai adventures with this level of training*
4	Primate
5	Tutelary
6	Principalin
7	Mentora
8	Scion-kai
9	Archmaster
10	Kai Grand Master

LORE-CIRCLES OF THE MAGNAKAI

In the years before their massacre, the Kai Masters of Sommerlund devoted themselves to the study of the Magnakai. These skills were divided into four schools of training called 'Lore-circles'. By mastering all of the Magnakai Disciplines of a Lore-circle, the Kai Masters developed their fighting prowess (COMBAT SKILL), and their physical and mental stamina (ENDURANCE) to a level far higher than any mortal warrior could otherwise attain.

Listed below are the four Lore-circles of the Magnakai and the skills that must be mastered in order to complete them.

Title of Magnakai Lore-circle	Magnakai Disciplines needed to complete the Lore-circle
CIRCLE OF FIRE	Weaponmastery & Huntmastery
CIRCLE OF LIGHT	Animal control & Curing
CIRCLE OF SOLARIS	Invisibility, Huntmastery & Pathsmanship
CIRCLE OF THE SPIRIT	Psi-surge, Psi-shield, Nexus & Divination

By completing a Lore-circle, you may add to your COMBAT SKILL and ENDURANCE the extra bonus points that are shown below.

Lore-circle bonuses

	COMBAT SKILL	ENDURANCE
CIRCLE OF FIRE	+ 1	+ 2
CIRCLE OF LIGHT	0	+ 3
CIRCLE OF SOLARIS	+ 1	+ 3
CIRCLE OF THE SPIRIT	+ 3	+ 3

All bonus points that you acquire by completing a Lore-circle are additions to your basic COMBAT SKILL and ENDURANCE scores.

IMPROVED DISCIPLINES

As you rise through the higher levels of Magnakai training you will find that your skills will steadily improve. If you are a Kai Master that has reached the rank of Primate (four skills), Tutelary (five skills), or Principalin (six skills), you will now benefit from the improvements to the following Magnakai Disciplines:

PRIMATE

Animal Control
Primates with this Magnakai Discipline are able to repel an animal that is intent on harming them by blocking

its sense of taste and smell. The level of success is dependent on the size and ferocity of the animal.

Curing

Primates with this skill have the ability to delay the effect of any poisons, including venoms, that they may come into contact with. Although a Kai Primate with this skill is not be able to neutralize a poison, he is able to slow its effect, giving him more time to find an antidote or cure.

Huntmastery

Primates with this skill have greatly increased agility and are able to climb without the use of climbing aids, such as ropes, etc.

Psi-surge

Primates with the Magnakai Discipline of Psi-surge can, by concentrating their psychic powers upon an object, set up vibrations that may lead to the disruption or destruction of the object.

Nexus

Primates with the skill of Nexus are able to offer a far greater resistance than before to the effects of noxious gases and fumes.

TUTELARY

Weaponmastery

Tutelaries are able to use defensive combat skills to great effect when fighting unarmed. When entering combat without a weapon, Tutelaries lose only 2 points from their COMBAT SKILL, instead of 4 points.

Invisibility

Tutelaries are able to increase the effectiveness of their skill when hiding from an enemy by drawing the enemy's attention to a place other than that in which they are hiding. The effectiveness of this ability increases as a Kai Master rises in rank.

Pathsmanship

Tutelaries with this skill can detect an enemy ambush within 500 yards of their position unless their ENDURANCE level is low due to a large number of wounds sustained or to lack of food.

Psi-screen

Tutelaries with this skill develop mental defences against magical charms and hostile telepathy. The effectiveness of this ability increases in strength as a Kai Master rises in rank.

Divination

Tutelaries who possess this Magnakai Discipline are able to recognize objects or creatures with magical skills or abilities. However, this improved Discipline can be negated if the creature or object is shielded from detection.

PRINCIPALIN

Animal Control

Principalins with this skill are able to call on a woodland animal (if nearby) to aid them, either in combat, or to act as a messenger or guide. The number of animals that can be summoned increases as a Kai Master rises in rank.

Invisibility
Principalins are able to mask any sounds made by their movements while using this skill.

Huntmastery
Principalins with this Magnakai Discipline are able to intensify their eyesight at will, giving them telescopic vision.

Psi-surge
Principalins using this skill in combat are able to confuse an enemy by planting seeds of doubt in its mind. The effectiveness of this ability increases as a Kai Master rises in rank.

Nexus
Principalins with this ability can extinguish fires by force of will alone. The size of the fire, and the number that can be extinguished using Nexus increases as a Kai Master rises in rank.

The nature of any additional improvements and how they affect your Magnakai Disciplines will be noted in the Improved Disciplines section of future Lone Wolf books.

MAGNAKAI WISDOM

Your search for the Lorestone of Tahou will be fraught with danger. The Darklords have launched a massive invasion into the freelands of Magnamund in a bid to take over the continent and thwart your Magnakai quest. Make notes as you progress through the story — they will be of great help in this and future adventures.

Many things that you find will help you during your adventure. Some Special Items will be of use in future Lone Wolf adventures and others may be red herrings of no real use at all, so be selective in what you decide to keep.

Choose your three Magnakai Disciplines with care, for a wise choice enables any player to complete the quest, no matter how weak his initial COMBAT SKILL and ENDURANCE points scores. Successful completion of previous Lone Wolf adventures, although an advantage, is not essential for the completion of this Magnakai adventure.

The future of Northern Magnamund now hinges on the success of this quest. May the spirit of your ancestors guide you on the path of the Magnakai.

Good luck!

1

A full moon lights the sky above Elzian on the evening you begin your journey to Tahou. Its ashen rays glimmer along the polished wooden outriggers that run the length of the hull of the *Skyrider*, and illuminate the crystal star ensign and the Sommlending flag as it flutters proudly from the mizzen-mast. The Elders of the High Council have gathered on the roof of their council chamber and, as you and Banedon climb the boarding ladder to the skyship, you pause to return their farewell salute. Bo'sun Nolrim, senior member of Banedon's crew of dwarves, welcomes you and his captain aboard. Surveying the craft, you notice that the *Skyrider* has changed very little since you were last aboard her, when you sailed the desert skies of Vassagonia in search of *The Book of the Magnakai*. The crew remember that voyage fondly and are justly proud of the part they played in the success of that perilous mission. 'Take the helm, bo'sun, and set a course for Navasari!' commands Banedon, as he leads you across the busy deck to his cabin at the prow.

Swiftly the lights of Elzian vanish as the *Skyrider* speeds into the night. A mile below, the jungle of Dessi and the barren peaks of the Xulun mountains race past beneath the keel, but in the comforting warmth of Banedon's cabin you feel no sensation of movement; only the hum of the powerful engine indicates how rapidly you are travelling. Over a delicious meal of salt beef and spiced fruit, Banedon explains the purpose of your journey to Navasari, a city that lies over a hundred miles south of Tahou. 'Our enemies are advancing across Magnamund like a tidal wave, destroying or carrying with them all in their path,' says the blond-haired magician, pointing to a map of the continent that adorns the cabin wall. 'Every day a new battle is being fought, and every day we lose another town or village to the Darklords. Before we venture into Tahou we must be sure that the city has not already fallen to Darklord Gnaag, lest we fly straight into a trap. I have many friends in Navasari, reliable friends, friends who are highly placed in the Senate of Anari. From them we will learn if the city still stands, and if it does, how long we can expect it to resist a Darklord assault.'

Mid-morning of the following day, the lookout catches a glimpse of Navasari as the *Skyrider* emerges from the Yajo Pass. Banedon takes control of the helm and steers the craft towards the east quarter of the city, landing it on the spacious roof of a magnificent, star-shaped building that overlooks the River Chah. A group of dignitaries, resplendent in high-necked robes of green and yellow silk, greet your arrival: these are some of the friends of whom Banedon spoke. Sadly they recount the grim course of events that has recently befallen their country. In the far north, the town of Resa was destroyed and its people massacred by an army of giaks. Two days later, a similar attack was launched by a Vassagonian army against the town of Zila. They swept along the Anari Pass, burning and looting every village through which they rode, and giving no quarter to those who dared resist them. And three days ago, on the western border, a fierce battle was fought at the Slovian town of Lovka for control of the bridge across the River Churdas. Shortly before midnight the might of Darklord Gnaag's horde fell upon the beleaguered garrison. They fought bravely, but by the dawn of the following day, all that remained of the town and its defenders were an acre of scorched earth and a cart full of charred bones. The three enemy armies are now advancing towards Tahou. President Toltuda, the head of state, has ordered the evacuation of all women and children from the capital, and has begun strengthening the city's defences to increase its chances of withstanding the impending siege. When Banedon tells of your intention to go to Tahou, one of his friends offers a few words of caution. 'It would be unwise to attempt a landing at the capital,' he warns. 'Heavy bolt throwers have been positioned on every rooftop and tower in case the city is attacked from the air. The Darklords captured Suentina in such a fashion and the Tahouese have learnt from their neighbour's misfortune. Skyships rarely visit Tahou, which makes it all the more likely that your craft would be mistaken for a hostile attacker.'

After long deliberation, you and Banedon decide to leave the *Skyrider* in Navasari and journey to Tahou by horse. Nolrim is left in charge of the craft and crew with instructions to wait here for your return. If Tahou is besieged and he has not received word from you after two weeks, he is to return to Dessi and report that your quest has failed.

Early next morning, you and Banedon climb into the saddles of two white Anarian steeds provided by his friends, and set off on your two-day ride to Tahou. Less than an hour after leaving Navasari you see a long line of wagons approaching. They are escorted by a troop of cavalry and each one is crowded with women and children.

If you wish to stop and question these people, turn to **126**.

If you wish to ride past them and press on with your journey, turn to **274**.

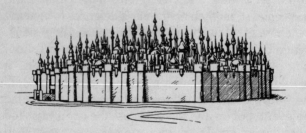

2

You look upon the city of Tahou from the balcony of a tall tower, the spire of the Thalis Temple, situated at the heart of the Rainbow Park. It is noon but there is no brightness in this day, for a grey blanket of smoke covers the sky. Below you lies a shattered city, its once proud buildings now seething infernos, its streets and squares choked with rubble. Hasty defences have been constructed where the city wall is holed or fallen, and the battlements to the north and east are covered with unburied dead.

Beyond the wall, the flats lie shrouded in a mist that curls like the smoke of a thousand campfires. Its thickness is unnatural and you sense at once that it has been conjured to hide the enemy. You leave the tower and make your own way through the burning streets towards the West District, where the fighting at the wall is fiercest. You pass the smouldering ruins of the Anarium and take a fire-swept street that leads to the West Gate. A building at the end of this street is being used as a shelter for the wounded. The roof has caught fire and a handful of soldiers are trying desperately to evacuate the wounded before it collapses.

If you wish to help these soldiers, turn to **342**.

If you wish to continue towards the West Gate, turn to **179**.

3

You leap from your hiding place like a tiger pouncing on its prey. Miraculously, the guard manages to parry your first blow but he is awestruck by your skill with a blade. He retreats towards the strongroom as you press your attack.

Strongroom Guard:
COMBAT SKILL 13   ENDURANCE 22

If you win the combat in less than three rounds, turn to **117**.

If you win but the combat lasts longer than three rounds, turn to **276**.

4

The shock of the fall and the numbing chill of the icy black water conspire to sap your strength. You flail and flounder in the deep until you are gripped by cramp and can no longer resist your doom. Unconsciousness smothers your pain as you sink slowly to the bottom of the lake, weighed down by your equipment and the freezing water that now fills your lungs.

Your life and your quest end here.

5

You have answered the riddle correctly and Khmar displays his collection of valuables from which you may choose your winnings. You may take any two of the articles listed; they are all Backpack Items:

    SILVER BOWL
    VIAL OF GOLD DUST
    ALTAR CLOTH
    SCROLL OF HONOUR
    JADIN ANKLET
    SPYGLASS

If you already carry the maximum number of Backpack Items, you may discard two of them in favour of your prize.

Since you have displayed your intelligence so effectively, the plains farmers are now reluctant to continue gambling. Khmar and his sons gather up their winnings and bid you goodnight, and the farmers follow suit.

If you wish to talk with the tavern owner, turn to **268**.

If you wish to order a meal, turn to **88**.

If you decide to call it a day and retire to your room, turn to **156**.

6

There is a faint click but the doors remain firmly closed. You press the lower three buttons at random in the hope of chancing on the correct combination, but the buttons lock into position and you cannot prise them up.

Turn to **207**.

7

You tie one end of the rope to the bottom rung and drop the rest into the darkness. Seconds later you hear it strike stone and you realize that you will not have too far to descend. As you climb down the rope, you pass through a layer of mist that glows with a curious blue-green luminescence. Twenty feet below the mist your feet touch firm ground. Close to where you land lie the skeletal remains of a human body.

If you wish to examine the body, turn to **186**.

If you wish to ignore it and investigate your surroundings, turn to **51**.

8

'Save your sympathy,' he sneers, ''cause you're about to meet him face to face!' Suddenly he lunges forward, a curved dagger gleaming in his hand. He flicks his wrist and the razor-sharp blade whips through an arc towards your throat.

If you have the Magnakai Discipline of Huntmastery, turn to **36**.

If you do not possess this skill, pick a number from the *Random Number Table*.

If the number you have picked is *0–3*, turn to **119**.

If it is *4–9*, turn to **260**.

9

Your arrow passes harmlessly beneath the creature's thrashing coils. There is no time to attempt a second shot. Quickly you shoulder your bow and draw a hand weapon, as it makes its diving attack.

Turn to **82**.

10

You are in combat with the Zakhan of Vassagonia. You cannot evade this combat and must fight him to the death.

Zakhan Kimah: COMBAT SKILL 34   ENDURANCE 40

He is immune to Mindblast and Psi-surge.

If you win the combat, turn to **350**.

11 – *Illustration I (overleaf)*

For countless hours you follow the great avenue as it bisects the heart of Zaaryx. The once-grand buildings that line this ancient thoroughfare are in varying states of decay: some are almost intact while others have disintegrated into little more than piles of black rubble. You try to keep track of time but it proves difficult in the perpetual half-light of this buried world. Twice you stop to sleep and eat (erase 2 Meals from your *Action Chart* or lose 6 ENDURANCE points) before you near the centre of the city. There you discover a great hall, its arched porticoes smooth and undamaged by time.

As you pass through one of these massive arches, you notice a group of reptilian creatures huddled at the top of a staircase that descends into darkness. They are stroking a large leathery egg and speaking to each other in a low hissing language.

If you wish to approach these creatures under cover of the pillars that line the hall, turn to **56**.
If you wish to call out to them, turn to **349**.
If you have a bow and wish to use it, turn to **171**.

12

You draw an arrow and take aim at a Giak's chest. He opens his yellow-flanged mouth to shriek for mercy but his cry is cut short as your feathered shaft pierces his heart. The other Giak rolls away from the body of his partner and scrambles to his feet, desperate to escape a similar fate. 'Aki-amaz!' he whimpers, hysterically, as he scurries towards the shadows of an alley.

I. A group of reptilian creatures are stroking a large leathery egg and speaking in a low hissing language

If you wish to fire your bow again, turn to **229**.
If you decide to let the Giak escape, turn to **57**.

13

You sift through the items heaped on the tables and disentangle the following, which could be useful:

> DAGGER
> ENOUGH FOOD FOR 3 MEALS
> ROPE
> FLASK OF WATER
> TORCH
> TINDERBOX
> BOW
> 3 ARROWS
> BLANKET
> SPEAR

If you wish to keep any of these items, be sure to make the necessary adjustments to your *Action Chart*.

Turn to **181**.

14

In the glare of your light you see the panel at the end of the passage loom into view. Damp green vines hang from the wall and it is not until you are within a few feet of the panel that you realize that the vines are not vines at all: they are the tentacles of a Roctopus that is nesting in the damp masonry.

If you have the Magnakai Discipline of Animal Control and have reached the Kai rank of Primate or higher, turn to **345**.
If you do not possess this skill, or have yet to reach this level of Kai training, turn to **32**.

15

Your mastery of Animal Control quickly restores the horse's usually calm temperament. You pat its neck affectionately and urge it forward, but still it refuses to move. You are about to use your skill to order it on when suddenly you see why it refuses to advance. The glistening head of a giant green serpent has slithered into view, its body still hidden by the tall crops. Its yellow tongue flickers hungrily between two sharp, venomous fangs and its cold black eyes watch your every move.

If you have a bow and wish to use it, turn to **216**.

If you wish to unsheathe a hand weapon in case it should attack, turn to **325**.

If you decide to shout a warning to Banedon, turn to **348**.

16

Snatching the seed from your pocket, you hurl it with all your strength at the gaping maw. The Fireseed splits open against a sabre-like fang and erupts in a sheet of flame, searing the creature's mouth and causing it to rear up in agony. With a loud, sickening crack, it slams its scaly head against the ceiling and falls, concussed, to the chamber floor.

With an energy born of desperation, you concentrate all your Kai skills upon opening the jammed lock. The intense concentration bleeds you of 2 ENDURANCE points but your persistence pays off.

Turn to **326**.

17

The guards are full of camaraderie and are surprisingly eager to help you find your way. 'Follow that street,' instructs the taller of the two, pointing across the lane, 'and take the first alley on the left. When you reach the Well of the Singing Serpents, turn right, and then take the second alley on the left. That will lead you straight to Chiban's house on Leech Street.' You thank them and accept a gulp of their boza wine before waving them farewell.

The soldier's directions prove to be accurate and in less than twenty minutes you find yourself standing in front of the magician's house in Leech Street.

Turn to **75**.

18

You dismount and hand Banedon the reins of your horse before approaching the door of the hut. With the tip of your weapon you lift the latch and push it open, wary of what may lurk inside, but the hut seems to be empty. It is furnished with a table, bed and chair, and a saucepan full of foul-smelling broth is simmering on the grate of a fire well charged with freshly cut logs.

If you have the Magnakai Discipline of Divination, turn to **143**.

If you wish to search the hut more thoroughly, turn to **265**.

If you decide to leave the hut and press on with your trek to Tahou, turn to **123**.

19

The mercenaries pocket the silver coins and you ask, 'Is a blond-haired Northlander being held here under arrest?'

'Not any more,' replies the bearded soldier. 'They carted him off to the Magistrates' Court about an hour ago.'

'The court's up there,' says the other man, pointing along the lane; 'Gallows Street, the first street on the left.'

Turn to **284**.

20

The Zakhan's mocking laughter is the last thing you hear as the fiery bolt of scarlet flame tears through your chest.

Tragically, you are slain here in Tahou, your life taken by the evil Zakhan of Vassagonia.

21

A startled shriek echoes through the deserted village as the riderless Kraan takes to the air. You watch as it crosses the river and flies towards the north before you turn your attention to the bodies of your dead foes.

If you wish to search the bodies for useful items, turn to **172**.

If you wish to leave and follow the track that leads out of the village, turn to **63**.

22

You draw an arrow and let fire at the leading creature. The shaft finds its grisly heart and the creature drops to the ground, its spindly arms thrashing fitfully. The others halt in their tracks and look down at their slain companion. You see a flicker of fear pass across their black, lifeless eyes.

If you wish to seize this opportunity to evade them by climbing the stairs, turn to **104**.

If you choose to draw a hand weapon in case they storm the hollow, turn to **71**.

23

At the end of the alley a signpost shaped like a heavy lance is embedded with its hilt in the ground. Three pointed placards are nailed to its shaft, pointing to streets that disappear into the tangle of smoky taverns and shops that crowd this part of Tahou.

If you have the Magnakai Discipline of Pathsmanship, turn to **337**.

If you wish to head north into Brooker Court, turn to **158**.

If you wish to go east into Eastwall Lane, turn to **250**.

If you wish to turn west into Varta Ride, turn to **278**.

24

You are unsheathing your weapon when you hear Banedon whisper; 'Follow me.' The rangers hear nothing, and as you drop the weapon their eyes follow it to the ground. At that instant, Banedon quickly recites the runes of a brotherhood spell and a flood of sticky fibres gush from his outstretched hand. The sergeant and a dozen of his men are caught in a net of gluey strands that hold them and their horses rooted firmly to the ground. Banedon spurs his horse at the startled few that have escaped his spell, and you follow closely on his heels. A handful of rangers pursue you along the highway, but your mounts are much faster and they soon give up the chase and return to their helpless comrades.

Only when the rangers and the standing stones finally disappear from sight, do you rein in your horses and slacken the pace.

Remember to erase one Weapon from your *Action Chart* before continuing your quest.

Turn to **213**.

25

Feverishly you tear open your Backpack and retrieve the vial. As soon as you swallow a handful of the blue pills you feel the pain in your lungs subside and a new wave of strength revitalizes your aching limbs. Oxygen is being drawn from the water around you, absorbed by your body through the pores of your skin. With determined strokes, you rise through the black water and break the surface. The distant shore gleams faintly in the dim half-light and you swim towards it as quickly as your frozen limbs will allow.

Aching and numb to the bone, you heave yourself out of the lake and collapse on the flat, spongy rocks that line the shore.

> If you have the Magnakai Discipline of Divination, turn to **298**.
>
> If you do not possess this skill, turn to **41**.

26

'Ha!' he snorts, contemptuously. 'So you are a student of magic, an apprentice in the mysteries of the arcane. How, pray tell, can one so gifted be unable to answer correctly such a simple question?'

With a flick of his hand he signals to his men on the parapet. It would be futile to attempt an escape from this murder hole and, reluctantly, you raise your hands in surrender.

Turn to **312**.

27

You draw your golden blade in time to deflect the bolt and send it screeching back down the staircase.

It explodes among the reptilians, destroying them and their weapon, and scattering their burning remains all over the corridor beyond.

Feverishly you fight to free your trapped leg, cutting at the barbs with the tip of the sun-sword. Eventually you succeed, and limp down the stairs as fast as your injuries will allow.

Turn to **241**.

28

The wretched beggars are overjoyed at your generosity and their grimy faces beam with delight as quickly they share out your gold. An old crone tugs at your sleeve and points with a crooked finger towards a small wooden hut set apart from the rest. She says it is the home of their shaman, the village holy-man. She offers to take you to him to receive a blessing.

If you wish to go with the old woman, turn to **180**.
If you decide to decline her offer and leave the village, turn to **52**.

29

Your Kai mastery enables you to recognize these pills; they are Sabito root tablets, made from compressed and powdered root of the Sabito plant. They enable the human body to absorb oxygen from water through the skin. Consequently anyone who swallows these pills will be able to 'breathe' underwater. The vial contains enough pills for two full doses.

If you wish to return to Brooker Court and continue on your way, turn to **334**.

If you wish to continue along the alley instead, turn to **278**.

30

You leap over the bodies of the dead Drakkarim and rush forward to plug the hole in the West Gate. Inspired by your heroic action, the scattered gate guards rally themselves and erect a makeshift barricade to seal the breach. When the door is secure you leave the West Gate and follow the battlements north towards the sound of renewed battle.

Turn to **168**.

31

The tunnel is narrow but there is sufficient headroom to allow you to enter on horseback. You lead the way, steering your nervous horse through the winding passage, which is lit by the glow of mine flies swarming in the roof overhead. Gradually the tunnel descends to a cavern where the floor is covered with puddles of milky liquid which bubbles up from fissures in the rock. Your horse lifts its head, sniffs the cool air and gives voice to a harsh neigh, alerting you to danger: in the distant shadows something alien is stirring.

Turn to **129**.

32 — *Illustration II (overleaf)*

Your light has awoken and angered the sleeping Roctopus, which uncoils its long, slimy tentacles swiftly from the wall. They surge towards you like a mass of wriggling snakes.

Roctopus:
COMBAT SKILL 18   ENDURANCE 18

II. The Roctopus uncoils its long, slimy tentacles

This creature is immune to Mindblast and Psi-surge. Owing to the confines of the passage, you must reduce your COMBAT SKILL by 2 points for the duration of the fight.

If you win the combat, turn to **139**.

33

As your light flares into life you notice an object lying on the steps. It was dropped by one of the reptilians as it made its hasty escape. It is a hexagonal-shaped piece of metal, embossed with a numerical design.

If you have seen and examined one of these hexagonal tokens previously in your adventure, turn to **161**.

If you have never examined one of these tokens before, you may look at this one; turn to **283**.

Or, you may leave it untouched and descend the stairs; turn to **130**.

34

Guyuk gives you each a key to your room and offers you both a glass of lovka on the house. Gratefully you accept and down the warming liquor in one gulp.

You notice that at the far end of your table a man sits with his two young sons. They appear to be gambling with a group of plains farmers seated opposite, although you can see no money changing hands.

If you wish to move along the table and sit next to them, turn to **339**.

If you wish to engage Guyuk in conversation, turn to **268**.

(continued over)

If you wish to order some food, turn to **88**.

35

Using your improved Kai mastery you focus on a distant tower, one of several that reinforce the city wall. This one marks the boundary between the city's North and West Districts, and as your vision magnifies, your suspicions are confirmed. Standing at the top of the tower is your companion, Banedon. You are relieved to know that he is still alive and resolve to make your way to the tower without delay.

Turn to **131**.

36

Your Kai mastery alerts you to the attack and you resist it with breathtaking speed. In one swift movement you unsheathe your weapon and lash out at your attacker, shearing off his arm at the elbow. Arm and dagger fall to the table and the soldier collapses screaming to the floor.

Shocked by what he has seen, his comrade kicks back his bench and retreats from the table. However, the drunken crowd goad him to retaliate and their gibes sting him into action. He pulls his blade free of its scabbard and leaps forward to attack.

Drunken Mercenary:
COMBAT SKILL 15 ENDURANCE 26

If you wish to evade combat, turn to **328**.
If you stay and win the fight, turn to **170**.

37

The hermit takes you back into the gorge and leads you to a place where a massive outcrop of rock overhangs a tangle of bushes and foliage. Hidden behind this leafy cover is the entrance to a cave. A rivulet of fresh water trickles from the cave mouth and the sound of constant dripping echoes in its distant depths.

'Follow the straight path through the cave. Do not stray from it. Soon you will emerge from the hills and see Tahou before your eyes. Godspeed.' And with that farewell wish the hermit hobbles away, eager to return to his hut and devour the fresh food you have given him.

Turn to **282**.

38

The ladder quickly gains momentum as you swing back and forth through the darkness. If you are to land safely on the narrow ledge you must time your jump to perfection.

Pick a number from the *Random Number Table*. If you have the Magnakai Discipline of Divination or Huntmastery, add 3 to the number you have picked.

If your total is now *0–4* turn to **317**.
If it is *5* or more, turn to **138**.

39

Using the cover afforded by the crowds, you escape across the precinct that surrounds the Senate House and enter a labyrinth of passages that disappear into a neighbourhood known as the Parish of Thieves. However, your escape has not gone completely unnoticed. From a tower of the Anarium, the Captain of the Senate Guard has been watching your getaway through his telescope, and he has despatched a troop of his best men to track you down.

On the corner of a dark alley you hear the sound of drunken laughter floating up from the battered door of an ale cellar. You turn away but the sudden tramp of booted feet echoing along the passage behind makes you change your mind. Quickly you descend the steps and take shelter in this lowly tavern.

Turn to **212**.

40

Gradually the tall fields of unripened wheat thin out as the land descends to the banks of the River Churdas. A long gravel beach lines the west bank, and on the other side, a quarter of a mile away, you see the rolling, treeless plains of Slovia stretching endlessly towards the horizon. You follow this mighty river upstream until you catch sight of a village in the distance.

If you have the Magnakai Discipline of Divination and have reached the rank of Primate or higher, turn to **199**.

If you want to take a closer look at this village, turn to **103**.

If you choose to avoid it, you must leave the river bank and ride back into the wheatfields; turn to **111**.

41

As your eyes become accustomed to the strange, blue-green half-light, you notice something unusual lying on the shore a hundred yards away. You approach cautiously and discover that it is the rope that once supported the cradle. The cradle itself now lies at the bottom of the lake, but a section of the rope fell to the shore. You examine it and discover that the end has been cut through with a sharp blade. The shock of this discovery sets your heart racing and you rack your brain, trying to think who would commit this act of deliberate sabotage. You know of only one who could have done such a ruthless deed.

Turn to **298**.

42

Using your Kai mastery you mimic the Tahouese dialect and try to persuade the commander that you have lived most of your life in the city. He looks at you suspiciously, but before he can ask you any questions that would be sure to catch you out, Banedon comes to your aid. 'We're students of Chiban the Magician,' he says, hurriedly. 'He lives at the Guildhouse on Leech Street, in the North District. He will vouch for us.'

The commander narrows his eyes. 'Bah!' he snorts. 'Let 'em enter. We need all the men we can get. Their blood's as good as any that'll be spilled in the defence of this city.'

Turn to **113**.

43

It is hexagonal in shape and made of a thin, creamy-coloured metal, which is engraved with the number '6'. (Make a note of this number in the margin of your *Action Chart*: it could prove to be useful later in your adventure.)

The metal begins to get hot and soon you can bend it with your fingers. Suddenly it bursts into flames forcing you to fling it aside before it burns your hand. The flaming token hits the lake and explodes in a cloud of white, powdery smoke. The echo of the explosion reverberates across the water and you turn to leave straight away in case it attracts more ghoulish inhabitants.

Turn to **175**.

44

Bravely you fight the mounted soldiers, but for every one you kill two more emerge from the gatehouse to take his place. Eventually you are overwhelmed by the sheer weight of their numbers, and as you weaken you are knocked down and trampled to death beneath their horses' hooves.

Your life and your quest end here.

45

The track takes you to the outskirts of a small river village. It looks deserted but as though the inhabitants have left in a hurry, taking nothing with them. A window shutter slams repeatedly in the distance, and you feel the chill of premonition as you ride along the empty cobbled street. As you approach the river wharf you suddenly hear new sounds, sounds that make you stop your horse dead in its tracks. You can hear the harsh voices of Giak soldiers.

Turn to **120**.

46 – *Illustration III (overleaf)*

Your caution is well placed. As soon as the door creaks open, a bolt of fiery energy screams over your head and explodes with a tremendous ear-splitting crack against the stairs behind. It was launched from a tube of glowing crystal, supported on the shoulders of two reptilians, kneeling in the corridor ahead. Their long jaws fall open in shocked surprise when they see you rise to your feet and run towards them, your weapon drawn ready to strike.

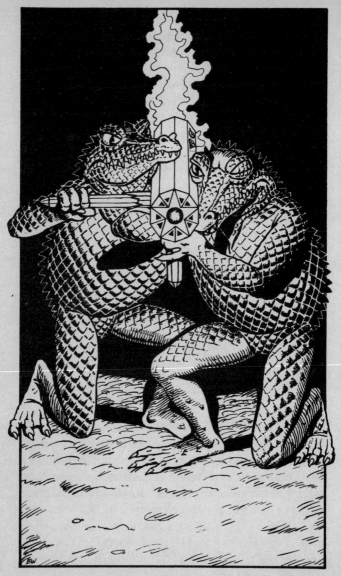

III.   Two reptilians kneel in the corridor ahead

Crocaryx:
COMBAT SKILL 12   ENDURANCE 38

These creatures are immune to Mindblast (but not Psi-surge). Owing to the speed of your attack, ignore any ENDURANCE point losses that you sustain in the first two rounds of combat.

If you win the combat, turn to **241**.

47

Over the years the dampness that pervades the prison has taken a heavy toll on the iron cell door. Using your Kai mastery, you are able to attack the lock mechanism by starting a vibration that shatters its corroded detent, the bar that holds the door shut.

Use of your psychic skill costs you 2 ENDURANCE points, but it frees you from the cell in less than a minute.

Turn to **185**.

48

A bolt of scarlet fire surges from the orb and speeds towards your head. You counter the attack but the bolt changes course in mid-flight, catching you off-balance. A searing pain tears into your arm as it glances from your shoulder and explodes somewhere in the street behind: lose 5 ENDURANCE points.

Turn to **128**.

49

Banedon helps you escape by casting a spell of levitation on the drunken soldiers. They·shriek with terror as suddenly they take to the air, floating upwards to crash into the soot-blackened rafters. The watching crowd finds this greatly amusing and you are able to run out of the room and escape along the street while they are helpless with laughter.

Turn to **146**.

50

Your answer is correct and Khmar is the first to congratulate your display of quick thinking as he returns the stake you lost. Having demonstrated your intelligence so effectively, the plains farmers are now reluctant to continue gambling. They gather up what little they have left and bid you goodnight. Khmar and his sons soon follow suit, leaving you and Banedon on your own.

If you wish to talk to the tavern owner, turn to **268**.
If you wish to order a meal, turn to **88**.
If you decide to call it a day and get some sleep, turn to **156**.

51

The ridged walls of the stone chamber narrow to a point where the mouth of a tunnel disappears steeply into the solid black rock. You enter the tunnel, taking care to control your descent as you slide towards a dim, flickering light that marks the end of the shaft. Halfway along the shaft you hear a rumble, like the sound of a distant earthquake. Then cracks appear in the roof and a deluge of dust and rubble pours down, choking and blinding you as it clogs your throat and eyes.

If you have the Magnakai Discipline of Nexus, turn to **118**.

If you do not possess this skill, turn to **291**.

52

As the hour of noon approaches, the rutted highway of khaki-coloured earth rises gently towards a flat-topped house near the horizon. Outside, at the entrance, is a three-legged stand erected over a fire made of ghorkas' dung. A battered tin pot full of soup hangs from the crotch of the stand and a group of farm hands stand in line waiting for the muddy liquid to boil. The smell of the fire is awful and it has to be blown on ceaselessly to prevent it from going out. Close to the house is a dirt track, which branches off the main highway and disappears to the west. A signpost, its wood cracked and twisted, points along the track. It reads:

TAHOU — 95 MILES

If you have the Magnakai Discipline of Pathsmanship, turn to **96**.

If you wish to follow the track, turn to **187**.

If you wish to question the farm hands, turn to **252**.

If you decide to continue along the highway, turn to **318**.

53

The rope shudders and instinctively you grab the rim of the cradle as it jerks violently to one side. Your knuckles whiten and cold sweat bathes your brow. The cradle swings and twists wildly, then a crack echoes in the darkness above as the rope snaps and you plunge headlong into the abyss.

Turn to **141**.

54

Arrogantly the sergeant-at-arms presents the case against you but Chief Magistrate Gwynian is unimpressed with his account of your crimes. 'Do you not know who it is that you have brought before this court?' he asks. The sergeant looks puzzled, and a thin film of sweat breaks out on his reddening face as his confidence begins to crumble. After a long and embarrassing silence he replies, 'Er . . . no, sir.'

'This is Lone Wolf, the last Kai Master of Sommerlund. Have you not heard of this man?'

'Yes, sir,' he replies, hoarsely, scarcely able to believe what he is hearing.

'I order his possessions be restored to him forthwith, and all charges against him to be dropped.'

A bell is rung to signify the end of the hearing and the courtroom is cleared. You are released from the cage and ushered into the Chief Magistrate's private chambers, where your equipment is returned to you. (Remember to erase the 'x' marks from your *Action Chart*.)

Turn to **76**.

55

The lane becomes narrower and gloomier as it climbs towards the East Gate. Marching down the hill comes a patrol of armed guards, led by an officer dressed in silvered mail. The moment he sees you he orders his men to load their bows. 'Surrender or die!' he shouts, as eighteen loaded bows are levelled at your heart.

If you wish to surrender to the patrol, turn to **192**.
If you wish to turn and run, turn to **211**.

56

The black flagstones are covered with a fine layer of grit that scrunches with every step you take.

If you have the Magnakai Discipline of Invisibility and have reached the Kai rank of Principalin, turn to **144**.
If you do not have this skill, or you have yet to reach this level of Kai training, turn to **349**.

57

As the rapid footfalls of the Giak recede, your basic Kai sixth sense warns you that he has recognized who you are. When he catches up with his unit and tells them what has happened here, they are sure to return *en masse*. Wisely you decide to leave; you remount your horse and follow the track that leads out of the river village.

Turn to **63**.

58

Standing beside the President's chair is a solid marble plinth with a bronze beacon — the Anarian symbol of law and order — fixed to the top. The President moves his hand to the padded arm of his chair and presses a button. All eyes are on the beacon. There is a flash of ignition and a jet of green flame roars upwards towards the domed ceiling.

'The Senate votes to aid your quest, Lone Wolf,' says Senator Zilaris. 'Come, we will escort you to the Square of the Dragons and make preparation for the Cauldron to be opened.'

The assembly is dissolved and the state coaches are summoned to take you and all the senators to the Tahou Cauldron. You share a carriage with the President, Senator Zilaris, and Senator Chil, who is anxious to apologize for opposing the majority vote. 'I trust you will forgive me, Lone Wolf,' he says, unctuously. 'I merely proposed what I thought was best for my country, but I now realize I was wrong.' You nod benignly, in the hope that he will cease his fawning. He smiles and turns to the President. 'Sir, I feel I must make amends for my misguided action in the Senate. If Lone Wolf is to enter the Cauldron tonight, surely it is our duty to ensure that he is adequately equipped. I propose that we visit one of my warehouses, where he is free to take anything he requires.'

58

The President agrees and the carriage is redirected to a warehouse near the Square of the Dragons. Senator Chil has many business interests in the city, and he supplies much of the weaponry and armour that equips the army. His warehouse is full of supplies and you are encouraged to take whatever you need. From the vast stores you select the following:

ROPE
SHORT SWORD
BLANKET
MACE
BOW
FLASK OF WATER
6 ARROWS
QUIVER
BROADSWORD
LANTERN
DAGGER

If you wish to keep any of the above items, remember to adjust your *Action Chart* accordingly.

Turn to **124**.

59

You start up the stairs but the first floor is already engulfed by flames. A gust of wind whips the fire down the stairwell, scorching your face and tunic (lose 2 ENDURANCE points) and forcing you to retreat into the street. Unable to help those who have been caught in the inferno, you leave the house sadly and hurry towards the West Gate.

Turn to **179**.

60

'Enter the Cauldron!' say the guards, incredulous. 'You're either a madman or you take us for fools.'

You try to explain but the guards become angry and refuse to listen. 'Dismount immediately!' they shout. 'You're both under arrest!'

If you wish to do as they command, turn to **312**.

If you wish to try to escape from the enclosure, turn to **72**.

61

You have taken less than a dozen steps when a terrible pain lances through your mind. A swirling cloud of mist engulfs your body and you are held in its paralysing grip. Unless you possess the Magnakai Discipline of Psi-screen and have reached the Kai rank of Tutelary or higher, lose 3 ENDURANCE points.

Gritting your teeth against the dreadful pain, you force yourself to turn and face your attacker as it runs forward to strike you down.

Turn to **301**.

62

The alley is dark and narrow but your basic Kai tracking skill enables you to follow the pickpocket as he makes his hurried escape. Suddenly he senses you are following him and dives into the side entrance of a large, three-storey building.

If you wish to follow him into the building, turn to **217**.

If you choose to call off the chase, you can walk back to Brooker Court and continue on your way; turn to **334**.

63

The track descends into a shallow valley, passes over a wooden bridge across a stagnant stream, and climbs towards the ridge of the hill. Passing over the crest, you come to a junction where the track joins a main highway. A whitewashed stone marker points to the left. It reads:

TAHOU — 90 MILES

You are hungry and must now eat a Meal or lose 3 ENDURANCE points.

To continue your journey to Tahou, turn to **145**.

64

Waves of pain course through your body and your head feels as if it is being squeezed in an invisible vice. You cry out as the psychic attack increases, paralysing your body and prising open the secrets of your mind: lose 5 ENDURANCE points. The man commands you to reveal the real reason you are here; you are powerless to resist his demand.

Turn to **305**.

65

'Well, that is most interesting,' answers the commander, sarcastically. 'Perhaps you can tell me when it was transported there from its previous location in the West District?'

With a flick of his hand he signals to his men on the parapet. It would be suicidal to attempt an escape from this murder hole; reluctantly, you raise your hands in surrender.

Turn to **312**.

66

As the last of the enemy fall to your murderous blows, you cut free your startled horse and leap into the saddle. Banedon gallops past, his loose robe billowing behind him like a pair of blue wings. Instinctively, you dig in your heels and urge your mount after him, fleeing the battleground, as yet more of the wolf-riders loom into view.

Turn to **293**.

67

The creature stretches its jaws and you stare with horror at a cavernous, fang-filled mouth. Desperately you look for a way to escape from this monster before it lunges and swallows you whole.

If you have a Fireseed, turn to **16**.
If you have a Psychic Ring, turn to **214**.
If you possess neither of these Special Items, turn to **277**.

68

You wait for the mercenaries to finish their pipe and go inside before daring to approach the barracks. You move like a shadow along the wall until you find a door that is unlocked and unguarded. It leads to the kitchens, where you manage to hide inside a store cupboard. There you eavesdrop on the conversations of the cooks while they prepare the evening meal. Their talk is mainly about the approaching enemy armies, and it is over an hour before you hear any mention of Banedon.

'At least we don't have to feed 'im now,' says one. 'They've taken 'im to the Magistrates' Court in Gallows Street. After what he's done I don't think he'll be getting a meal ever again!'

Your heart sinks upon hearing this. You climb out of the storeroom through a window and make your way back to Eastwall Lane.

If you wish to retrace your steps along the lane, turn to **278**.

If you decide to continue to follow the street east, turn to **284**.

69

Using your improved Kai mastery you focus on the distant dust cloud. It grows larger and sharper as your telescopic vision magnifies the image. You see a patrol of Anarian cavalry riding towards you, led by one who wears a crimson cloak. You count twenty lances, each of them bearing a small flag embroidered with the arms of Tahou.

If you wish to ride forward to meet these soldiers, turn to **193**.

If you choose to avoid them by hiding behind the standing stones, turn to **78**.

70

The instant the engineer leans forward to lay the plank

in place, you let loose your arrow. Unfortunately, the soldier who holds the screen sees its approach and moves to intercept it. The shaft sinks harmlessly into the leather-covered screen and the bridge is completed with two blows of the engineer's hammer.

'Shaag Drakkarim!' scream the Drakkar assault-troopers as they blow a hole in the West Gate.

If you wish to help defend the West Gate, turn to **220**.

If you decide to stay on the battlements, turn to **249**.

71

Slowly the ghouls slink away until their forms merge with the shadows at the far side of the lake. One of their number has been crouching above the entrance to the hollow, waiting to drop on you at the first opportunity, but, on seeing its kin disperse, it decides not to remain any longer. As it jumps down from the step above an odd-looking token falls from the pocket of its tattered jacket. It tries to retrieve it but you step forward and strike a blow that lays open its stringy grey hand, and the accursed creature scurries away hissing ghoulish obscenities.

If you wish to examine this token, turn to **43**.

If you prefer to leave it and hurry away from the hollow in case the ghouls decide to return, turn to **175**.

72

Your boots thump your horse's ribs and he responds by surging forward, scattering the angry guards. You tug the reins and steer him towards the open gate through which the guards entered the enclosure, but he is hit in the neck by a crossbow bolt fired from above, and he shrieks and stumbles. An alarm bell clangs and furious shouting echoes in your ears as you tumble from your dying steed. Suddenly a pain explodes in your shoulder − you have been hit by a bolt. Pick a number from the *Random Number Table* and add 2 to the number you have picked. The total is equal to the number of ENDURANCE points you must lose as a result of your wound.

It is futile to continue your escape attempt; you are caught like fish in a barrel. Painfully you raise your hands in surrender.

Turn to **312**.

73

Your decision to discard half your equipment proves to be a fatal error of judgement. The amount of weight you have jettisoned is not enough to help you rise to the surface before cramp afflicts your aching limbs. Unable to resist your doom, you sink slowly to the bottom of the lake, weighed down by your Backpack and the water that now fills your lungs.

Your life and your quest end here.

74

Shielding his eyes from the sun, Banedon surveys the horizon. After a few minutes he shakes his head. 'No tracks or highway, nor even a sign of habitation for that matter. To get a better view we need to reach higher ground, but as there are no trees or hills in sight I'll have to improvise.'

And with that he whispers the runes of a brotherhood spell. Slowly he rises from the saddle until he is hovering in the air over twenty feet above your head. Then, having scoured the surrounding countryside, he descends slowly as the effects of his levitation spell begin to wear off.

'There's a river on the horizon,' he says, slipping his feet back into the stirrups. 'It's probably the Churdas. Over to the right, about five miles away, there's a small village on the river bank.'

If you wish to ride towards the river, turn to **40**.
If you wish to veer right and ride towards the village, turn to **111**.
If you choose to turn around and retrace your tracks to the junction, turn to **222**.

75 – *Illustration IV*

It is a grand building of polished red stone set with small, diamond-paned windows. You pass beneath its arched gateway and climb the tiled steps that lead to the front door. Twice you rap the twisted iron knocker and wait expectantly for the portal to creak slowly open. Minutes later it swings back to reveal two men standing in the doorway. One is the grey-haired aristocratic figure of Chiban, the other, to your utter astonishment, is your companion Banedon.

'Lone Wolf!' says the young magician, his voice filled with surprise and delight. 'You're free, but how?'

'I could ask the same of you, Banedon,' you reply, with a smile.

IV. In the doorway stand the grey-haired aristocratic figure
of Chiban, and your companion Banedon

'I heard of my former pupil's arrest and made arrangements for his release. We were discussing how to secure your freedom but it would appear that such plans are now unnecessary,' explains the aged Chiban, gently closing the great oak door. He turns his kindly gaze to you and says, 'I am honoured to meet you, Kai Lord. Banedon has told me of your quest. I have knowledge of that which you seek and I shall aid you all I can so that you may recover it.'

The master magician beckons you both to follow him to his study. The room is filled with massive wooden racks of books and papers, and at its centre a large circular table stands completely covered with the implements of his magical researches. He clears a space amid this clutter and motions you to sit. 'You must both be famished after your journey and your ordeal. Come, eat and enjoy.'

For a few seconds a shimmering pool of light fills the space, then it fades, leaving a sumptuous meal in its wake. If you have lost any ENDURANCE points on your adventure so far, you may now restore 3 points as you consume the delicious food.

Turn to **269**.

76

'The Elder Magi sent word of your coming, Lone Wolf,' says Gwynian. 'They knew of my appointment to the city judiciary when I came to live here two years ago. My home, the Halls of Learning in Varetta, was destroyed by a fire set by agents of the Darklords. Like yourself, I am a sole survivor, the last of my order. The Elders asked me to afford you what protection I could and to help you in your quest for the Lorestone of Tahou.'

He leads you to a table, the surface of which is engraved with a huge map of the city. With a rod of glass he points to the location of the Tahou Cauldron: it is in the Square of the Dragons in the West District of the city. 'The Cauldron is a funnel-shaped hollow with a circular shaft at its base. The shaft descends to the ruins of the ancient city of Zaaryx, 500 feet below Tahou. Legend tells us that the Lorestone was thrown into the Cauldron to prevent the Black Zakhan of Vassagonia from capturing it during the Great Khordaim War. The shaft was closed off and has remained sealed for the last 360 years.'

You ask Gwynian if he can order the release of your companion. 'It has already been done,' he replies. 'I released Banedon into the custody of his former mentor, Chiban the Magician, three hours ago. He is with him now at his house on Leech Street. He is quite safe, but you must not delay your quest any further by going there yourself. At dawn the enemy will be at the gates of the city and the battle for Tahou will have begun. There is only one man that can help you now, for there is only one person that can grant you access to the shaft of the Cauldron that descends to Zaaryx. That man is President Toltuda of Anari. Come, I will arrange an audience with him immediately.'

Turn to **105**.

77

You detect that these creatures have the ability to communicate telepathically, although it is one of their less developed skills. Their leader appears to be a female, she is taller and lighter in colour than the rest. You take the risk of calling to her telepathically, and she responds by turning to face you. When her companions see what has attracted her attention they shriek with fear and scurry down the stairs, carrying with them the egg, which they cradle protectively in their webbed hands. But she remains and speaks to you with her mind. 'You are unlike the other man-things that have ventured into our domain. What is it that you seek? Care you not what happens to those of your kind who trespass here?' The reptilian points to the far end of the hall, where a group of ghouls are huddled in the shadows. Your skin creeps as you realize they were once men like you.

'I seek the Lorestone,' you reply, boldly. 'I am the Kai Lord Lone Wolf and I quest for the wisdom of Nyxator that I may vanquish the spawn of his enemies and save my people from destruction.'

Her harsh gaze softens as your proud words fill her mind. You sense a sadness within her, but she replies with words of joy. 'Your quest will be fulfilled, as it was by your sire many centuries ago. We have waited long for your coming, Skarn, and we will fulfil our duty to He that gave us life.'

Without an outward sign she beckons you to follow her and you comply without hesitation.

Turn to **200**.

Turn to **200**.

78

There is only one group of standing stones that offers enough cover for you, Banedon, and your mounts, and they are situated very close to the highway along which the cavalry must pass.

You wait tensely as the thunder of their hooves grows steadily louder. Then, suddenly, your horse rears up, startled by a snake, which has slithered around its foreleg.

If you have the Magnakai Discipline of Animal Control, turn to **167**.

If you do not possess this skill, turn to **290**.

79

The evil blade crackles and spits as you draw it from your belt. A flicker of fear in the Zakhan's eye tells you that he recognizes the weapon you wield and knows that it has the power to penetrate his energy shield.

If you wish to throw the dagger at him, turn to **239**.

If you wish to engage him in hand-to-hand combat, turn to **10**.

80

The eating house is crowded with soldiers. They sit at benches drawn up to long oak tables or sprawl around a log fire that crackles in a broad stone grate. Your entrance causes them to pause in their noisy conversations as they look you up and down. However, their curiosity is soon satisfied and they return to their feasting and boasting.

'This way, gentlemen,' beckons the owner, and leads you through the crowd to a table in the corner of the high-ceilinged room. Banedon hands him a clutch of silver Lune and the jolly red-cheeked man waddles away to fetch you food and ale. The soldiers are dressed in a variety of uniforms, many of which you recognize to be the tunics of mercenary regiments from the Stornlands. Two of these soldiers of fortune share your table. They talk in hushed tones and cast nervous glances at another group of men sitting near the fire.

If you wish to talk to these soldiers, turn to **292**.
If you decide to say nothing while you wait for your food, turn to **102**.

81

In spite of your fatigue your reactions are lightning fast. You regain your grip in an instant and raise your foot to steady yourself against the jagged outcrop. Then, as soon as the ladder ceases to twist like an angry snake, you continue your descent.

Turn to **173**.

82 — *Illustration V*

You are in combat with a deadly predator of the Anarian plain. Owing to the speed of its attack, you cannot avoid fighting.

Anarian Sky-snake:
COMBAT SKILL 23   ENDURANCE 28

This creature is immune to Mindblast and Psi-surge. Double all ENDURANCE point losses you sustain due to its venomous fangs and claws. Unless you possess the Magnakai Discipline of Huntmastery, reduce your COMBAT SKILL by 2 points for the duration of the combat.

V. You are in combat with a deadly predator of the Anarian plain, the Anarian Sky-snake

If you win and the fight lasts four rounds or less, turn to **247**.

If the fight lasts longer than four rounds, turn to **151**.

83

'Lay down your weapon, mortal, for I have power enough at my command to blast you to sightless atoms!' The reptilian raises her webbed hand and from the darkness of a dozen arches protrude tubes of glowing crystal, each one charged with a pulse of destructive energy that is aimed at you. 'Tell me what draws you here, lest my patience fail!' she demands.

Reluctantly you sheathe your weapon and obey her command.

Turn to **256**.

84

You focus on the guard and launch a pulse of psychic energy at his brain. He has no defence against such an attack and his entire body immediately begins to shake violently. Four seconds later he lapses into unconsciousness.

Turn to **165**.

85

You draw a hand weapon just in time to parry the sergeant's attack. His blade glances away and he curses your speed as you duck his sweeping backstroke. With a growl he pulls his horse away and orders six of his men to cut you down.

Anarian Rangers:
COMBAT SKILL 32   ENDURANCE 38

If you have the Magnakai Discipline of Animal Control, add 2 to your COMBAT SKILL for the duration of the combat.

If you win the combat, turn to **176**.

86

You stare unblinkingly into his cruel, dark eyes. Suddenly he lunges forward, a curved dagger gleaming in his hand. Its razor-sharp blade speeds towards your throat but you counter his attack in an instant with a savage swipe that shears his arm off at the elbow. Arm and dagger fall to the table and the soldier falls screaming to the floor. His comrade kicks back his bench and steps away as he fumbles for his sword. With a drunken yell he whirls the heavy blade around his head and leaps forward to attack.

Drunken Mercenary:
COMBAT SKILL 15   ENDURANCE 26

You wish to evade combat, turn to **328**.
If you stay and win the combat, turn to **170**.

87

At last the grisly creature surrenders to death and collapses at your feet. You sheathe your weapon and kneel over its torn body, drawn by the sight of a ring on a finger of its right hand. It gleams incredibly, as though only minutes old, and the deep yellow stone that is set in the silvery metal glows with an eldritch light.

If you wish to keep this Psychic Ring, mark it on your *Action Chart* as a Special Item that you keep in your pocket.

(continued over)

Turn to **11**.

88

A serving girl ushers you into an adjoining room, where smoke from an open charcoal fire spirals up to the roof, filling the air with its pungent aroma. You seat yourselves at a round oak table and the girl brings two plates loaded with broiled ghorkas steak and roasted parsnips. Two tankards of ale serve to wash down the feast which Banedon, in a generous mood, pays for with twelve silver Lune.

Having satisfied your hunger and revived your strength (you may restore any ENDURANCE points lost on your adventure so far), you bid Banedon goodnight and retire to your room.

Turn to **156**.

89

You land heavily among the rocks and debris, gashing open both knees and your chin before rolling to a halt at the base of the tower wall (lose 4 ENDURANCE points).

If you have survived the jump, you enter the tower; turn to **131**.

90

You run from the staircase as quickly as you can and follow a corridor that heads towards the front of the Anarium. In the distance you can see an entrance hall teeming with people, and two soldiers, both armed with halberds, standing on guard with their backs towards you. To your left there is a window and you look through to see your carriage parked close to the side of the building.

If you wish to escape through the window, turn to **149**.

If you wish to escape along the corridor, turn to **121**.

91

There is no time to choose which equipment to keep and which to throw away.

Count up the number of Backpack Items you possess and, if there is an odd number, erase the last one on your list. Divide this list in two and mark one with an 'H' and the other with a 'T'. Now take a coin and flick it in the air. If the coin shows 'heads', erase all the items on the 'H' list. If it shows 'tails', erase all the items on the 'T' list.

Once you have made the necessary adjustments to your *Action Chart*, pick a number from the *Random Number Table*. If you have the Magnakai Discipline of Nexus, add 4 to the number you have picked.

If your total is now *0–4*, turn to **73**.

If it is *5* or more, turn to **246**.

92

You enter the pass side by side, galloping your white Anarian steeds along the rubbish-strewn road that winds its way through the deserted settlement. As you pass the watchtower, a chilling howl rises from the shadows behind the huts. Then, like demons from a nightmare, a host of snarling Giaks bursts into view, riding from their hiding places astride giant doomwolves. They thunder towards you on either side, shrieking and thrusting their spears at the darkening sky.

Pick a number from the *Random Number Table*.

If the number you have picked is *0–4*, turn to **293**.
If it is *5–9*, turn to **257**.

93

As the massive body of the Zadragon crashes lifelessly to the floor of the chamber, you turn and run back to the door, where you concentrate all your Kai skills upon freeing the jammed lock. The intense concentration bleeds you of 2 ENDURANCE points before your persistence pays off.

Turn to **326**.

94

The alley is dark and narrow. You draw on all your Kai skills to scour the inky blackness ahead, but you can detect no movement among the ramshackle houses.

If you have a Kalte Firesphere, a Torch and Tinderbox, or a Lantern, turn to **194**.
If you do not possess any of these items or do not wish to use them, turn to **311**.

95

'Cut him down!' shouts the sergeant, pointing at you with his axe. The soldiers release their taut bow-strings and two blue-feathered arrows scream towards your chest.

Pick a number from the *Random Number Table*. If you have the Magnakai Discipline of Huntmastery, add 2 to the number you have picked. If you have completed the Lore-circle of Solaris, add 3.

If your total is now *0–3*, turn to **125**.
If it is *4–8*, turn to **309**.
If it is *9* or more, turn to **238**.

96

Immediately you sense that the signpost is pointing in the wrong direction. Tahou lies to the north, yet this signpost is pointing towards the River Churdas in the west.

If you wish to ignore the signpost and continue along the highway, turn to **318**.
If you wish to question the farm hands, turn to **252**.

97 — *Illustration VI (overleaf)*

You are awoken by the stench of decay. A grey-skinned being, squatting on its haunches, stares down at you with grim, inhuman eyes. Drool trickles from its ragged lips and the rusty sword it holds in its twisted, man-like hand is lifted to kill.

Zaaryx Ghoul: COMBAT SKILL 19   ENDURANCE 27

Owing to the surprise of this attack you cannot make use of a bow. Unless you possess the Magnakai Discipline of Huntmastery, deduct 3 from your COMBAT SKILL for the duration of the fight.

If you win the combat, turn to **338**.

VI. The Zaaryx Ghoul stares down at you with grim,
inhuman *eyes*

98

'Hold there!' booms the mercenary leader. 'We've a debt to settle.' He flips his cloak aside to show his sword in its scabbard and motions two of his men to the door to cut off your escape. The protests of the hall owner go unheeded as the leader draws his sword and signals his men to attack.

Deldenian Mercenaries:
COMBAT SKILL 26   ENDURANCE 34

If you wish to evade the combat after one round, turn to **223**.

If you stay and win the combat, turn to **174**.

99

The Drakkarim assault-troopers crouch behind their oblong shields, waiting for their chance to storm the gate. You draw your arrow and take aim at the engineer's screen. You will have only a second in which to fire as he steps forward to slip the final plank in place.

Pick a number from the *Random Number Table*. If you have the Magnakai Discipline of Weapon-mastery with Bow, add 3 to the number you have picked.

If your total is now *0–6*, turn to **70**.

If it is 7 or more, turn to **198**.

100

Tahou, an ancient stronghold containing a vast city, is a formidable and wondrous sight in the moonlight, the imposing walls and towers of red stone and grey rock assume the softening sheen of velvet, and the city is often referred to as 'The velvet fortress'. Beyond the towers and high curtain wall you can see a thousand spires and minarets, grouped as thickly as the trees of a forest. Tiny lights twinkle in countless windows and portals, adding to the splendour of the mighty capital.

Near to the city's South Gate, the highway is flanked by beacons which illuminate those who approach the gatehouse. A drawbridge spans a moat of black water and, as you ride across, a bell tolls from the portcullised archway ahead.

'Two civilian riders at the South Gate,' yells a soldierly voice.

'Raise the postern,' shouts another.

There is a clatter of chains and a scraping of stone. You watch the portcullis, expecting it to rise, but it does not move. Instead, a narrow portal opens at the base of the wall and an armoured guard steps from the shadows. He motions you to enter and you follow Banedon along a corridor of stone, leading to a secure enclosure. You glance upwards to see the faces of a dozen soldiers, peering down at you from behind a parapet that encircles the high enclosure walls. All of them grasp loaded crossbows which they train on you as you move. Then a small gate creaks open and two guards appear, armed with broad-bladed spears.

'Who are you?' one demands in a gruff tone. 'Why do you seek entry to Tahou?'

If you have an Invitation and wish to show it, turn to **321**.

If you wish to tell the guards that you have come
    to offer your services in the defence of the city,
    turn to **196**.

If you wish to say that you intend to enter the
    Tahou Cauldron, turn to **60**.

101

Pulses of psychic energy leap from the gem, washing
over you in waves that leave you shaking and
breathless. Your Psi-shield protects your nervous
system but you are unable to stop the pulses from
penetrating deep into your mind. The man
commands you to reveal the real reason you are here.
Steadily he increases the force of his mind-gem until
you can no longer resist.

Turn to **305**.

102

Four muscular mercenaries, all wearing tunics of
emerald green leather emblazoned with the owl's head
crest of Delden, rise from their seats near the fire and
stare coldly in your direction. They point at the
soldiers on your table, curse loudly, and then strut
across the crowded hall, barging aside anyone that
gets in their way. The two soldiers break out in a
sweat and glare at each other fearfully.

'Treacherous scum!' spits the leading mercenary,
grabbing them both by the collar and hauling them
to their feet. 'A thousand Lune went missing from
the regiment's pay chest the night you two were
supposed to be guarding it. Neither o' you have got
brains or guts enough to steal it yourselves, so who
was it, eh?'

The soldiers are scared out of their wits. They have no idea who stole the money, but they know their leader will have them flogged to death unless they tell him what he wants to know. In desperation one of the men points a trembling finger at you and Banedon. 'It was them . . . they did it, they did it!'

If you wish to deny this false charge, turn to **127**.

If you wish to avoid a confrontation by leaving the eating house, turn to **98**.

If you wish to draw a weapon in case the mercenaries attack you out of hand, turn to **308**.

103

The approach to the village is deserted: it is as if its inhabitants have simply dropped everything and left in a great hurry. A window shutter slams repeatedly in the breeze and a rusty sign, hanging by chains from a warehouse beam, squeaks like a hungry rat; they are the only sounds you hear as you advance cautiously along the narrow, cobbled wharf. As you reach the corner of the warehouse you stop your horse dead in its tracks. You can hear the harsh voices of Giak soldiers.

Turn to **120**.

104

As you step from the hollow a weight drops on to your back and drags you to your knees. Long, sharp fingers, as hard as steel, clamp around your throat and the sound of gnashing fangs fills your ears. You twist and roll, hoping to break from the creature's grip, but its hold is unnaturally strong.

Ghoul: COMBAT SKILL 18   ENDURANCE 29

Reduce your COMBAT SKILL by 3 points for the duration of the fight unless you possess the Magnakai Discipline of Huntmastery or Divination.

> If you win and the fight lasts three rounds or less, turn to **228**.
> If the fight lasts longer than three rounds, turn to **322**.

105

Gwynian dispatches a messenger to the Anarium, the House of the Senate, where members of the governing council have gathered for an emergency assembly called by the President himself. Within the hour, the messenger returns with a furled parchment bearing the presidential seal. 'He has agreed to hear your plea, Lone Wolf,' says Gwynian, his eyes scanning the official reply. This news raises your flagging spirits but the sage seems a little disappointed.

'I was hoping for a private audience with the President,' he says, 'but in view of the current crisis, I suppose it is the best we can expect. You must appear before the Senate this evening, and state your reasons for wishing to enter the Tahou Cauldron. They will consider your request and vote accordingly. Their decision will be final.'

He hands you the scroll and arranges for his personal carriage to take you to the Anarium. As you climb aboard and sink into the plush, upholstered seat, you exchange a farewell wave with Gwynian the Sage. 'May the gods watch over you,' he says, 'and may you live to fulfil your destiny.'

Turn to **300**.

106

The seed explodes with a flash and illuminates the staircase with its vivid yellow flame. Halfway down the stairs you notice an object that was dropped by one of the reptilians as it made its hasty escape. It is a hexagonal piece of metal, embossed with a numerical design.

If you have seen and examined one of these hexagonal tokens at a previous stage in your quest, turn to **161**.

If you have never examined one of these tokens before, you may look at this one; turn to **283**.

Or you may leave it untouched and descend the stairs; turn to **130**.

107

A gurgling scream echoes from the alleyway – your arrow has found its mark. Seconds later the Giak staggers into view, its arms thrashing wildly as it tries to grab hold of the shaft buried deep in the middle of its back. In desperation, it draws a dagger from its boot and attempts to throw it at you, but a wave of pain engulfs the creature at that moment and the vicious blade slips harmlessly from its grasp. With one last curse it swoons and drops lifelessly to the ground.

If you wish to search the bodies of the slain Giaks, turn to **172**.

If you wish to leave and follow the track that leads out of the village, turn to **63**.

108

The wagon races along the rubble-strewn street towards a tower, one of many that reinforce the city wall. Standing at the top of the tower is your companion, Banedon. You ask the captain to stop and let you speak to your old friend, but he refuses even to slow down. 'I must reach the North Gate without delay!' he bellows, and whips the horses to increase their speed.

If you have the Magnakai Discipline of Divination, turn to **272**.

If you wish to jump off the wagon as it passes the tower, turn to **230**.

If you choose to stay on the wagon and go to the North Gate with the captain, turn to **340**.

109

'We're both students of Chiban the Magician,' says Banedon, hurriedly trying to defuse the situation. 'He lives at the Guildhouse on Leech Street in the North District. He will vouch for us.'

'Hold your tongue!' snaps the commander at your startled companion. 'I want your friend to tell me something about this city, the city that he is prepared to lay down his life for.' He moves nearer and stares at you icily. 'In which district of Tahou is the Cauldron to be found?'

You know that the city is divided into four districts each named after a point of the compass, but you cannot recall in which district the Cauldron lies.

> If you choose to answer, 'The North District', turn to **26**.
>
> If you choose to answer, 'The South District', turn to **65**.
>
> If you decide to answer, 'The West District', turn to **255**.
>
> If you wish to answer, 'The East District', turn to **178**.
>
> If you decide to give no answer at all, turn to **333**.

110

This narrow thoroughfare descends to a maze of broken streets and dank passages that carry traffic to and from the city's North District. Guided by your basic Kai tracking skill, you wend your way through the dingy lanes until you arrive finally at Leech Street and the house of Chiban the Magician.

Turn to **75**.

111

Your passage through the wheatfields is slow and laborious. Drainage ditches, cut seemingly at random, criss-cross the plain. They ensnare your horse's hooves causing him to stumble and fall. Twice you are thrown and on the second occasion you gash your head badly on a jagged rock – lose 3 ENDURANCE points.

Later, by chance, you happen upon a cart track that crosses the plain from left to right.

> If you wish to follow the track to the left, turn to **45**.

If you wish to follow the track to the right, turn to **63**.

If you have the Magnakai Discipline of Divination and have reached the rank of Primate or higher, turn to **262**.

112

The last thing you see is the huge stone ball as it falls on you.

Tragically, you lose your life here at the siege of Tahou.

113

A guard pushes open the enclosure gate and motions you to leave. You are free to enter the city but your horses are impounded. You protest and demand that they be returned, but to no avail. 'Order of the Senate,' says the commander, offhandedly, 'an emergency decree. All horses belonging to the civil population must be delivered into the care of the garrison stables until the state of emergency is lifted.'

Reluctantly you allow the guards to take your steeds and, as they are being led away, the commander hands you each a piece of vellum stamped with a date and a number. 'Receipts for the horses,' he says, his tone noticeably more friendly.

You pocket the Receipt (mark this on your *Action Chart* as a Special Item that you keep in your pocket; owing to its size you need not discard another item in its favour if you already have your maximum number of items) and are about to walk away when he calls out, 'Report to the citadel first thing in the morning. You'll be allocated your battle positions for when the enemy attack.'

Turn to **242**.

114

With determined strokes you rise through the black water and break the surface, coughing and gasping for air. At first the incredible coldness stunned your senses, but now it revives them and spurs you to swim towards the distant shore, gleaming faintly in the half-light.

Aching and numb to the bone, you heave yourself out of the lake and collapse on the flat, spongy rocks that line the shore.

If you have the Magnakai Discipline of Divination, turn to **298**.
If you do not possess this skill, turn to **41**.

115

It is the father's turn to ask a riddle, but firstly you must decide on your stake. You can choose to gamble either one Special Item or three Backpack Items. If you should fail to answer the riddle correctly you will forfeit the item (or items) you have staked. If you answer the riddle correctly you will win the chance to pick any two items from the father's hoard of valuables. Put a tick on your *Action Chart* beside the item or items that you wish to stake.

A hush descends as you wait for the riddle patiently. The father, whose name is Khmar, draws his dagger from its scabbard and lays it on the table. Then he rests his hand on the shoulder of his eldest son and says, 'This dagger is now half as old as my son Loen was when the dagger was new. Loen is now fifteen years old. How old is the dagger?'

If you think you can answer the riddle, turn to the entry number that is the same as the answer.
If you cannot answer the riddle, turn to **204**.

116

The reptilians see a glint of light reflected in the mirror and they discharge their weapon at the gap in the door. Only the speed of your reflexes saves you from death as a bolt of energy explodes with a deafening noise, showering you with sparks and fragments of stone. Wiping the grit from your eyes, you seize the chance to attack the reptilians. As you emerge from the blackened hole in the door, their long jaws drop open in shocked surprise.

Crocaryx: COMBAT SKILL 12   ENDURANCE 38

These creatures are immune to Mindblast (but not Psi-surge). Owing to the surprise of your attack, ignore any ENDURANCE losses that you sustain in the first two rounds of combat.

If you win the fight, turn to **241**.

117

The guard receives a fatal wound to the heart. He gasps, his sword slipping from his fingers as he crashes lifelessly to the floor.

Turn to **177**.

118

Your Magnakai Discipline enables you to filter air from the massive dust cloud without inhaling any of the harmful grit. The cloud contains spores of a fungus that is deadly to humans, but your Kai skill shields you from these perilous microscopic cells.

Turn to **233**.

119

The vicious blade pierces your skin but you pull away instinctively, saving yourself from a far more serious wounding: lose 3 ENDURANCE points.

Drawing blood has made the mercenaries over-confident. They advance around the table, cursing and taunting you with their knives.

Drunken Mercenaries:
COMBAT SKILL 18   ENDURANCE 30

If you wish to evade combat, turn to **49**.
If you stay and win the combat, turn to **170**.

120 — *Illustration VII*

Silently you slip from the saddle and peer around the corner. In the middle of the street beyond, a

VII. Two Giak scouts are loading their booty on to the
back of a Kraan

company of Giak scouts are sifting through items they have looted from the village. Two of the evil creatures are loading their booty on to the back of a Kraan, a large, black-winged creature, while the others cram their ill-gotten gains in their pockets and packs. What they cannot carry they delight in despoiling, leaving behind a trail of filth and debris in the buildings they have ransacked.

'Oka der!' shouts their officer, brandishing a long, black sword with a jagged edge. 'Akamaza ek!' His greedy soldiers are reluctant to obey his commands, but a few blows with the flat of his blade quickly change their minds. Muttering and snarling, they scurry off into a side alley, reappearing a few minutes later astride large, grey wolves. 'Rekenara kluz!' growls the officer, and the pack ride out of the village, heading north along the bank of the River Churdas.

The Kraan and its two riders take to the air but the beast is so overburdened with loot that it cannot clear the rooftops. Frantically it beats its leathery wings, hovering erratically just a few feet off the ground. The Giaks urge it on with kicks and punches but to no avail. Suddenly it lurches forward and the Giaks tumble headfirst on to the cobblestones a few feet from where you stand. 'Orgadaka!' they cry, as they catch sight of you and Banedon hiding at the corner.

If you have a bow and wish to use it, turn to **12**.
If you wish to attack the Giaks with a hand weapon before they have a chance to stand, turn to **285**.
If you choose to avoid combat by remounting your horse and galloping along the track that leads out of the village, turn to **63**.

121

The sound of your running feet is lost amid the noise and bustle of the crowded hall, and the guards do not hear you as you sprint towards their backs. All they see is a blur of green as you duck under their crossed halberds and disappear into the teeming throng.

Turn to **39**.

122

Fearfully you approach the shadow until you can discern its gruesome features. It is a ghoul, similar to those you encountered in the hollow, but this creature looks even less human. Its swollen skull is set lopsided on its withered frame, and the long black tongue that hangs from its jagged mouth drips with a sticky black venom that bubbles like boiling acid as it hits the ground. It raises a wasted hand and a cone of mist whirls towards your chest.

If you possess the Magnakai Discipline of Psi-screen, turn to **203**.
If you do not possess this Kai skill, turn to **191**.

123

A rough dirt track leads away from the hut and into the hills above. It is a precarious path to follow, especially on horseback and at dusk. Only your quick wits and Kai skills keep you and your horse from plunging into the steep-sided gullies that border the rocky track.

124

Eventually you arrive at a junction, where the path meets a wider road heading north and south. A signpost lies shattered on the ground, but instinctively you know that the north route leads to Tahou. You point the way and Banedon acknowledges your signal with a wave. As you turn on to the highway you suddenly feel that you are being watched. Pinpoints of red fire glint in the darkness and the sound of hungry, panting doomwolves comes to you on the night air. Before you can shout a warning, a shrill scream splits the night – it is the chilling sound of a Giak battle-cry. You are being attacked.

Turn to **244**.

124

In addition to your supplies, Senator Chil provides the winch, ropes and cradle by which you will be lowered into the shaft that descends to Zaaryx. Upon your arrival at the Square of the Dragons he supervises the assembly of these vital components, while you stand with Senator Zilaris and stare in awe at the Cauldron itself.

In the glow of a hundred lanterns it takes on the appearance of a huge, steep-sided sink that is stoppered with a plug of stone. The key to this plug is a rod of Korlinium that, until this evening, was kept locked in the vaults of the Anarium. Now it rests in the hands of the President. Senator Chil signals that his work is complete and the President inserts the crystal rod into the plug of ancient stone. At first nothing happens. Then you sense a vibration beneath your feet. Crackling tongues of pale blue fire lap the rim of the plug and the hiss of escaping air breaks the seal of three centuries' grime that holds the plug in place. Levers and ropes are brought into action and slowly the great block is lifted and the shaft to Zaaryx uncovered.

Turn to **205**.

125

The deadly arrows pierce your heart and stomach. Pain engulfs you like a raging fire but a chilling numbness soon follows, washing over you like a wave of soothing balm. You fight to stay on your feet but darkness encroaches on all sides: it is the cold embrace of death.

Your life and your quest end here.

126

The officer in charge of the mounted escort rides forward to meet you. He wears silvered Anarian mail and a winged helmet embossed with the crest of Tahou.

'Hail, captain!' says Banedon, upon seeing his crown-shaped badge of rank. The man narrows his eyes and regards you both with suspicion. He is about to reach for his sword when a woman shouts from the leading wagon.

'Banedon! Banedon! Is that you?'

Your companion recognizes the woman and returns her wave. 'Lortha! By the stars, I had not expected to meet you here,' he says in a surprised tone. The captain relaxes his guard and motions to the wagons

127

to move on, anxious that his entourage is not delayed on the highway.

'You can fall in with us or save your reunion till we reach Navasari,' he says, curtly, and rides on without waiting for a reply.

'Lortha is the wife of Chiban, a famous Tahouese magician. He was my mentor when I lived and studied in the city,' says Banedon.

If you wish Banedon to talk to this woman, turn to **209**.

If you insist that you both continue your journey without delay, turn to **274**.

127

'They are lying,' you say, your voice calm yet forceful. 'We have never seen these men before.'

'We have only just arrived in the city,' says Banedon. 'We know nothing about your missing gold.'

Contemptuously, the mercenary leader hurls the trembling men aside and reaches for his sword. 'We too have only just arrived. Our silver was stolen during our march here.' He steps back a pace and draws his blade. 'Take 'em, lads!' he cries, and leads the attack.

Deldenian Mercenaries:
COMBAT SKILL 26   ENDURANCE 34

If you wish to evade combat after one round, turn to **223**.

If you stay and win the combat, turn to **174**.

128

The Zakhan gloats over your pain and moves forward to exploit his advantage. You grit your teeth and raise your sword to defend yourself against his attack. You are aware of the Zakhan's troops fighting a desperate battle at the West Gate, and you know that you must defeat him or the city will be lost.

Zakhan Kimah: COMBAT SKILL 44   ENDURANCE 50

He is immune to Mindblast and Psi-surge.

If you win the combat, turn to **350**.

129 – *Illustration VIII (overleaf)*

In the depths of the tunnel a glistening form is slowly slinking into view. Gnarled plates like armour encase its barrel chest, and lidless slit-pupilled eyes stare coldly from beneath its ridged forehead. A low, grating rumble issues from its fanged mouth as it increases its pace and makes ready to pounce.

Cave Leekhon: COMBAT SKILL 27   ENDURANCE 38

This creature is immune to Mindblast (but not Psi-surge). Unless you possess the Magnakai Discipline of Animal Control, reduce your COMBAT SKILL by 2 points for the duration of the combat.

If you win the fight, turn to **169**.

130

Cautiously you descend the staircase, expecting the unexpected, your weapon held ready in case the reptilians attempt a surprise attack. The glow of your light washes over the black stone stairs below and you freeze in your tracks when you notice a poorly

VIII. The glistening form of the Cave Leekhon slinks into
view

concealed trap. Carefully you step over the snare and continue towards a door at the bottom of the stairs. It is unlocked and slightly ajar.

If you have a Mirror, turn to **237**.

If you wish to push open the door and continue, turn to **324**.

If you wish to push open the door and flatten yourself to the floor, in case the reptilians have prepared an ambush for you, turn to **46**.

131

The iron door to the tower is unlocked and you enter unopposed. At the top of the steep stone steps you find a ladder to a trapdoor. Quickly you climb the ladder and emerge on to the roof. 'By the gods!' exclaims Banedon, when you appear. 'My prayers have been answered. You are alive, Lone Wolf. You are alive!' Tears of joy fill his eyes as he welcomes your return warmly.

He and his mentor Chiban have been viewing the siege from this vantage point for the last three days. From this position they control the movement of the few reserves allocated to the north and west city walls, using them to fill in the gaps where the enemy's attacks have weakened the defences. Banedon recounts how the siege has progressed; how twice the enemy have broken into the city and been repelled by the determined defenders. Attacks from the air have set the city ablaze, but the enemy have lost great numbers of their flying Kraan and now they are too weak to dare use the few that remain. The Anarium was destroyed in the first few hours of the siege and many senators lost their lives, including Senator Chil and President Toltuda.

Then he asks of your quest and is overjoyed to hear of its success. 'The gods smile on you, Lone Wolf. So long as you live there is hope for us all.'

Turn to **258**.

132

'I'll not have you sleeping in the stables, old friend!' says Banedon, as he flicks open his money pouch. He hands the tavern owner twenty-four freshly minted Lune, and in return Guyuk gives you each a key to your room and offers you both a glass of lovka on the house. Gratefully you accept and down the warming liquor in one gulp.

You notice that a man and his two young sons are sitting at the far end of your table. They appear to be gambling with a group of plains farmers seated opposite, although you see no money change hands.

If you wish to move along the table and sit next to them, turn to **339**.

If you wish to engage Guyuk in conversation, turn to **268**.

If you wish to order some food, turn to **88**.

133

Your Kai mastery alerts you to a trap set immediately ahead. The surface of one of the stairs is thin and conceals a shallow box lined with barbed hooks. If you were to tread on the stair, your foot would shatter the cover and become ensnared among the hooks, incapacitating you and injuring your foot severely.

Carefully you step over this trap before continuing down the stairs.

Suddenly you are bathed in a white light that emanates from holes in the stone ceiling, and at once you see the bottom of the staircase twenty yards ahead. There is a door at the foot of the stairs and it is slightly ajar.

If you have a Mirror, turn to **237**.
If you wish to push open this door and continue, turn to **324**.
If you wish to push open the door and flatten yourself to the floor in case the reptilians have prepared an ambush for you, turn to **46**.

134

The iron door slams shut and you are left alone to contemplate your unfortunate arrival in Tahou. The cell is narrow and damp, with patches of mould that discolour the red stone walls. The uneven floor is strewn with filthy, mouldy straw and the stale air is heavy with the stench of rotting food and sewage. A solitary window is criss-crossed with bronze bars, green with age, and below it a thousand scratches record the passing days of another visitor that fell foul of the gatehouse guard. Anxiously you cast your eyes around this filthy prison, searching for a chink in its armour that could lead to your escape.

If you have the Magnakai Discipline of Psi-surge and have reached the Kai rank of Primate or higher, turn to **47**.
If you have the Magnakai Discipline of Nexus, turn to **202**.

(continued over)

If you possess neither of these skills, turn to **227**.

135

Amid chaos and confusion you leave the ale cellar through a concealed door in the wall of the arch. It opens on to a sloping passage that descends to a tunnel lit by oil-soaked torches fixed at random along the tiled walls. A foul smell assails your nostrils – the unmistakable stench of an underground sewer. You follow Sogh along a narrow ledge that runs parallel to a sluggish sewage channel, taking care not to slip on the slime-encrusted tiles. After a few minutes, he halts beneath one of the spluttering torches and presses its rusty iron bracket. There is a grating rumble and a section of the tunnel wall opens to reveal an amazing sight.

Turn to **243**.

136

The burly sergeant snatches the parchment from your hand and studies it carefully. Without raising his head he asks how two Northlanders came to possess a personal invitation to one of Tahou's most respected households. When Banedon explains your meeting with Lortha, and how he was once a student of Chiban, her husband, the sergeant somewhat reluctantly accepts your story and returns the Invitation. 'Stay on the highway and make sure you reach Tahou by sunset,' he says, as he signals to his troop to let you pass. 'Enemy scouts have been sighted in the hills south of the capital. If you're not inside the city walls by nightfall . . . ' He draws his finger quickly across his throat.

You thank him for his advice and watch as he and his troop wheel away and ride south. You pocket the Invitation and glance apprehensively at Banedon before pressing on with your own journey north.

Turn to **213**.

137

A bronze beacon, the Anarian symbol of law and order, is fixed into a plinth of marble that stands beside the President's chair. He moves his finger to a button on the arm of the chair and all eyes turn to stare at the beacon. There is a flash of ignition and a jet of red flame roars upwards towards the domed ceiling. 'Seize him!' shouts Senator Chil. 'Seize Lone Wolf!'

The President has voted against you and now the Senate guards are closing in on all sides to arrest you. In a single bound you leave your seat and sprint along the gallery towards an empty staircase. To your right a guard is rushing to intercept your escape. He is unarmed but he has a net with which he hopes to ensnare you. He casts it as you are about to descend the stairs.

Pick a number from the *Random Number Table*. If you have the Magnakai Discipline of Huntmastery, add 1 to the number you have picked. If you have completed the Lore-circle of Fire, add 2.

If your total is now *3* or less, turn to **182**.
If it is *4* or more, turn to **236**.

138

With the grace of a panther you leap from the swinging ladder and land safely in the centre of the narrow ledge. You advance along this rubble-strewn shelf of black stone, following it as it descends through a layer of swirling mist that glows with a faint blue-green luminescence. Below the mist lies a chamber; its walls are scarred with deep furrows, as if it was excavated from solid rock by a huge clawed hand.

Close to the wall lies what appears to be a large bundle of rags. But as you approach them you suddenly realize that they are more than simply rags: they contain the skeletal remains of a human body.

If you wish to examine the body, turn to **186**.
If you wish to ignore it and explore the chamber, turn to **51**.

139

'The lever that opens the exit panel is near the ceiling,' whispers Sogh, casting nervous glances over his shoulder. He can hear the guards scratching at the wall behind, trying to locate the brick which opens the concealed entrance. Your fingers find the lever and you pull it. The panel slides aside and you both step out into an empty horse stall. As the panel slides back into position, you jam it with a piece of timber. Fortunately the stables are empty of guards and it is easy to make your escape through a side window that gives access to an alley.

'Good luck, Northlander. I hope you find your friend. Remember, they have him locked up at the Eastgate Barracks,' says Sogh. You bid him farewell and as you watch him disappear into the shadows, you consider your best course of action.

> If you decide to make your way to the Eastgate Barracks, turn to **23**.
>
> If you decide to seek the help of Chiban the Magician, Banedon's former teacher, turn to **221**.

140

Using your Kai skill you concentrate and focus your telescopic vision on the distant horizon. Gradually the image magnifies until you can see clearly that the glimmer is a wide, fast-flowing river. Your basic Kai sense of tracking tells you it is the River Churdas.

> If you wish to continue your ride towards the River Churdas, turn to **40**.
>
> If you wish to retrace your tracks to the highway, turn to **222**.

141

You fall like a stone into the whirling blackness. In desperation you thrust out your arms, hoping to seize an outcrop or ledge, but there is nothing in the void for you to grasp. The freezing wind screams past your face and your senses are overwhelmed by the horror of your impending doom. Suddenly an icy shock engulfs you as you strike the surface of a lake and plunge into its lightless depths. Stunned by the sudden impact and numbed by the icy water, you sink several fathoms before you can muster your strength and strike out for the surface.

Pick a number from the *Random Number Table*. If you have the Magnakai Discipline of Nexus, add 4 to the number you have picked.

If your total is now *0–3*, turn to **114**.
If it is *4–7*, turn to **289**.
If it is *8* or more, turn to **4**.

142

The courthouse of the Chief Magistrate is a grim, grey building. Devoid of any decoration or embellishment, its stark bare walls serve to remind the Tahouese of its sober purpose. It is a place where justice is meted out to wrong-doers. Harsh punishments are imposed: floggings and executions take place here every day of the week. All trials are conducted before a magistrate and his decision is final as there are no juries in Tahou. The Chief Magistrate presides over crimes that are serious enough to warrant the death penalty, and your heart sinks when you learn that he is to sit in judgement of you.

You put up quite a struggle but your shackles prevent you from breaking free of your armed escort. They drag you into the courtroom and throw you face down into an iron cage that stands before the Chief Magistrate's chair. A bell is struck to signal the arrival of the Chief Magistrate and he enters the court surrounded by an entourage of scribes. The bell rings once more and the scribes say with one voice, 'This session is now in hearing.'

If you have ever visited the city of Varetta or a hut on the Ruanon Pike, in a previous Lone Wolf adventure, turn to **294**.

If you have never visited either of these places, turn to **54**.

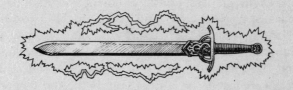

143

You detect that someone is hiding in a cellar, located directly below where you are now standing. Access to this hiding place is via a trapdoor in the far corner of the hut, close to the fireplace.

If you wish to open the trapdoor and demand that the person show himself, turn to **206**.

If you choose to ignore the trapdoor and search the hut instead, turn to **190**.

If you wish to push the bed across the trapdoor, thereby sealing it, turn to **225**.

144

Using your improved mastery, you move forward silently pillar by pillar until you are within a few feet of the creatures. Their heads resemble those of baby crocodiles, but their bodies and forelimbs are toad-like and covered with hard, shiny scales. They chatter incessantly and, judging by their behaviour and speech patterns, they are sentient beings.

> If you possess the Magnakai Discipline of Divination, turn to **77**.
>
> If you do not possess this skill, turn to **313**.

145

The afternoon passes swiftly as you ride across endless miles of treeless grass land. You stumble upon no village or hamlet and spend the hours listening to Banedon's account of recent events in Sommerlund and the Lastlands. Three years have passed since you were last in the land of your birth, and you are hungry to hear all that has transpired since then.

It is an hour past sunset and night is drawing its black cloak around you when you see a flickering red light on the road ahead: it is the village of Chadi. A great fire roars in the hearth of Guyuk's Tavern in Chadi, inviting the travel-sore to stop and warm their weary bones. You decide to stay overnight and, as soon as you have stabled your horses, you enter the tavern to ask the price of a room. The taproom is suprisingly quiet. It is full of villagers and farmers but they are a sullen crowd, content to sit in silence and brood over their glasses of lovka, a strong Slovian rye spirit named after the town where it was first distilled.

Guyuk the tavern owner greets you with a nervous nod of his shiny bald head and shows you to a table. There are no bars or counters in Anarian taverns; instead, the customers sit at long banqueting tables and wait for the owner and his staff to serve them. He smiles uneasily as he answers your enquiry about a room. 'A single room with a bed would be twelve Lune each.'

> If you have enough money to pay for a room (twelve Lune equals four Gold Crowns), do so, and turn to **34**.
>
> If you do not have sufficient Lune or Gold Crowns to pay for a room, turn to **132**.

146

Soon you arrive at a part of the city that Banedon remembers well. It borders a large public garden called the Rainbow Park, so named because of the vast number of rare and colourful flowers that grow there. The park is now an encampment for those who have answered the President's desperate call for defenders. Survivors from the towns of Resa and Zila have joined forces with green-clad Daroga woodsmen, tough hill-dwellers from the Chah mountain valley, and river-folk from the Churdas, forming regiments to reinforce the Tahou garrison. Their battle-stained banners, lit by the flickering glow of a hundred camp fires, flutter above the tents that fill the great park.

Opposite the entrance stands the Guildhall of Tailors. You turn into an avenue running beside this imposing hall, then cross into the North District by means of alleys and side streets, and finally emerge at Leech Street, just opposite the house of Chiban the Magician. His is a grand building of polished red stone set with small, diamond-paned windows that twinkle like cat's eyes in the moonlight. You pass beneath its arched gateway and climb the magnificent tiled steps that lead to a black oak door. Banedon raps the knocker and you wait patiently for it to open.

Minutes later the great door swings aside and the aristocratic figure of Chiban stands framed in the doorway. Keen-eyed and grey haired, he welcomes you both with surprise and delight.

'Banedon!' he exclaims, like a father reunited with a long lost son. 'How good it is to see you. But what brings you to Tahou at this darkest of hours? Have you come to offer your skills in the defence of our beleaguered city?'

'My services are yours to command, my lord Chiban,' answers Banedon, bowing respectfully to his former mentor. 'Yet also I return to your esteemed household to seek your help at the behest of King Ulnar of Sommerlund. May I introduce my companion — Lone Wolf.'

Chiban turns his kindly gaze on you and smiles knowingly. 'I am honoured to meet you, Kai Lord,' he says. 'I have knowledge of that which you seek and I shall aid you all I can in your search for it.'

He beckons you to enter and the door closes behind you seemingly of its own accord. You follow Chiban to his study. The musty room is lined with massive wooden racks full of books and papers. At its centre a large, circular table is completely covered with the implements of his magical researches. He clears a space amid the clutter and motions you to sit. 'You must both be famished after your journey here. Come, eat and enjoy!' For a few seconds, a shimmering pool of light fills the space, then fades, leaving a sumptuous meal of grilled trout, baked potatoes, hakeroot and sparkling Anarian wine.

If you have lost any ENDURANCE points on your adventure so far, you may now restore 3 points as you consume this delicious meal.

Turn to **269**.

147

You are covered in the blood of your foes. The stench is so unbearable that you have to wash in the lake before you can go any further. When you return to the hollow to collect your Backpack, you notice an odd-looking token lying next to one of the dead ghouls.

If you wish to examine this token, turn to **43**.
If you choose to ignore it and leave this place, turn to **175**.

148 – *Illustration IX (overleaf)*

The doomwolf breathes its last but its claws remain hooked in your saddle. You strive to cut it away but your horse can no longer bear its weight. With a neigh of terror his legs buckle and you are thrown to the blood-soaked ground. Before you can regain your feet, you are set upon by the snarling Giak horde.

6 Doomwolves and Giak Riders:
COMBAT SKILL 38   ENDURANCE 56

You must fight these creatures as one enemy. Owing to your fall, reduce your COMBAT SKILL by 2 points for the first two rounds of combat.

If you win the combat, turn to **66**.

IX. You are set upon by the snarling Giak horde

149

The window is bolted shut. If you are determined to escape this way you will have to take the risk of jumping through a pane of thick glass.

If you still wish to escape through the window, turn to **266**.

If you choose to escape along the corridor instead, turn to **121**.

150

A warm tingling runs through your body as the Lorestone descends into your hands and, as you touch the crystal, your senses become charged with a new vitality that obliterates the fatigue of your ordeal and fills you with new-found wisdom and strength (restore your ENDURANCE score to its original total).

Then a swirl of colour engulfs your body and you feel yourself fall forward into the throat of a spinning vortex. The chamber dissolves and you begin to rise at an ever-increasing speed, as if you were falling upwards. A surge of light makes you close your eyes, but it passes in an instant and you find yourself staring down at an incredible and terrible sight.

Turn to **2**.

151

As the sky-snake rears to avoid your blow, Banedon steps forward and launches a bolt of lightning from his open hand. The pulse of energy tears into the creature's neck, almost severing its head from its body as it sends it spinning into the tall crops. Wiping the sweat from your brow, you thank your companion for a most effective helping hand.

Turn to **247**.

152

A deafening roar fills the stairwell as a bolt of raw energy hurtles from the rod. You stare aghast as it speeds towards your chest and explodes with a splash of colour that is the last you will ever see.

In the council chamber of the Elder Magi in Elzian, the golden torch flickers and dies. The members of the High Council hang their heads in sorrow for they know that your life and their hopes have ended here in Zaaryx.

Your quest is over.

153

The gap between each rung measures approximately one foot, and you gather in over 400 rungs before reaching the end of the ladder. The thought of having to descend such an enormous depth fills you with dread, but your desire to find the Lorestone overcomes this fear. You feed the rope ladder back into the void and begin your descent.

Turn to **231**.

154

As you kneel by the trapdoor, your basic Kai sense of hunting reveals to you that someone is hiding in the cellar below. Carefully you raise the trapdoor and demand that the person show himself to you.

If you decided to keep any of the items you discovered in the hut, turn to **232**.

If you did not keep any of the items, turn to **206**.

155

You search the clothes and backpack of the dead pickpocket thoroughly and retrieve your stolen property. You also discover the following items which the thief has hidden about his person:

> DAGGER
> ENOUGH FOOD FOR TWO MEALS
> 28 LUNE (equivalent to 7 Gold Crowns)
> BLANKET
> VIAL OF BLUE PILLS

If you wish to keep any of the above items, remember to amend your *Action Chart* accordingly.

If you have the Magnakai Discipline of Curing, you can identify the Blue Pills: turn to **29**.

If you wish to return to Brooker Court and continue on your way, turn to **334**.

If you wish to continue along the alley instead, turn to **278**.

156

The room, which overlooks the courtyard and stables, is small yet surprisingly clean and comfortable. You sleep well but you are rudely awoken at dawn by the clang of a brass hand-bell. Guyuk's wife is walking around the courtyard ringing it for all she's worth. 'Daybreak, daybreak! All awake, all awake!' she cries, her voice only slightly less piercing than her bell. Quickly you wash and dress before gathering together your equipment and heading for the stables. Banedon is already there, having risen before dawn to prepare the horses.

The sky is cloudless and the air is warm and still as you ride out of Chadi. Open grasslands stretch before you, broken occasionally by the low, whitewashed farm buildings and peasant dwellings. It is noon when you arrive at a mass of standing stones that line the highway approaches to the village of Phea. Banedon recalls a local legend that the Black Zakhan of Vassagonia once came to wage war on the defenceless inhabitants of Phea, who had no army. The besieged people offered up prayers to the goddess Ishir, who was sufficiently moved by their plight to cause the wicked Vassagonians to become petrified right where they stood, clad in full armour and clasping their weapons. It strikes you that the Pheans may very soon have cause to pray for Ishir's help a second time.

A mile beyond the village you see a cloud of dust on the highway.

> If you have the Magnakai Discipline of Huntmastery and have reached the rank of Principalin, turn to **69**.
> If you do not possess this skill or have yet to reach this Kai rank, turn to **240**.

157

You dress your wounds as best you can before advancing along the rubble-strewn ledge. You descend through a layer of swirling mist that glows with a faint blue-green luminescence. Below the mist lies a chamber; its walls are scarred with deep furrows, as if it was excavated from the solid rock by a huge clawed hand.

Close to the wall lies a bundle of rags. As you approach it you suddenly realize that the skeletal remains of a human body are contained within the rags.

If you wish to examine the body, turn to **186**.
If you wish to ignore it and explore the chamber, turn to **51**.

158

Your passage along Brooker Court is hampered by the companies of militiamen that march to and from the centre of the city. The majority of them are oafish peasants, hastily armed with spear and sword, and bullied into a semblance of soldierly order by guardsmen from the Tahou garrison. You wait in shadowy doorways and allow them to pass before continuing on your way towards the city's North District.

You are nearing the end of Brooker Court when a man dressed in an ill-fitting tunic staggers drunkenly out of a tavern and collides with you. 'Shorry!' he hiccups, and wanders off along an alley to your left.

If you have the Magnakai Discipline of Divination
or Huntmastery, turn to **201**.

If you do not possess this skill, turn to **273**.

159

You focus your improved Kai mastery at the flames
that engulf the top of the staircase. Within a few
seconds they flicker and die, allowing you to reach
the first floor in safety. The captain is crouched over
his brother, protecting him with his body from the
fiery debris that is raining down from the roof. Swiftly
you pull him to his feet and motion him to help carry
his wounded brother out of the house. As you reach
the street below, the roof collapses and the whole
of the first floor is swallowed by flame.

'We owe you our lives,' says the captain, gratefully,
as his men load his brother on to an open-backed
wagon. 'I must return to my command at the North
Gate – will you join me? I would be honoured to
fight by your side.'

If you wish to go with the captain to the North Gate,
turn to **108**.

If you choose to decline his offer, you continue
along the street towards the West Gate; turn to
179.

160

Your senses tingle with a premonition of danger –
you are sure that the watchtower and huts conceal
an enemy, lying in ambush. You tell Banedon your
fears and he looks ahead, his keen eyes narrowing,
but the pass is dark with the gathering dusk and he

cannot detect anything unusual about the settlement, except that it appears deserted.

'If we avoid the pass, we'll have to make a wide detour and rejoin the highway at a place deeper in the hills,' he says, scanning the shadowy highlands. 'Even if we don't get lost, we'll be lucky to reach Tahou before nightfall.'

> If you wish to avoid the settlement and make a wide detour, turn to **335**.
> If you decide to gallop through the pass, despite the risk of an ambush, turn to **92**.

161

With the experience of what happened when you last touched one of these strange tokens still fresh in your mind, you avoid picking up this one. However, this does not stop you from looking at its intricate design. This token is engraved with a mathematical equation and you calculate the answer to be 320. (Make a note of this number in the margin of your *Action Chart*, beneath the number you already have listed, as it may well prove useful at a later stage of your adventure.)

Turn to **130**.

162

Once again you come face to face with the sergeant. He curses and strikes you across the cheek with the hilt of his sword, leaving you stunned and bloodied: lose 2 ENDURANCE points.

You are dragged back to your cell and four armed guards are placed outside the door with orders to shoot to kill if you should attempt another escape.

Turn to **227**.

163

Deduct from your *Action Chart* however many Gold Crowns (or Lune) you wish to give to the poor villagers.

If you give them three or more Gold Crowns, (twelve Lune), turn to **28**.

If you give them less than three Gold Crowns, turn to **235**.

164

At once you recognize Sogh, the thief who helped you escape from the South Gate tower. 'Hail, Northlander,' he says, a wide grin spreading across his mouse-like face. 'So we meet again. What prompts you to visit the Purple Purse ale cellar?'

Before you can reply, the door bursts open and in rush six heavily armed Senate House guards. Thinking that the ale cellar is being raided, something of a routine event here at the Purple Purse, the shady patrons drop their drinks and flee towards the open door in an attempt to escape arrest. Sogh grabs your sleeve and points to a shadowy archway. 'Time to leave,' he hisses. 'Follow me.'

Turn to **135**.

165

Sogh looks at the guard then looks at you in awe. 'How did you do that?' he asks, incredulous. 'No time to explain,' you reply, as you scramble out from beneath the stairs and move towards the unconscious guard.

Turn to **177**.

166

As you draw closer you can make out the gruesome features of the shadow. It is a ghoul, similar to those you encountered at the lake, but this creature looks even less human. Its swollen skull is set lopsided on its withered frame and its tongue drips with a sticky black venom. It raises a wasted hand and launches a whirl of mist towards your chest, but your psychic defence disperses this evil swirling cloud. The creature howls with frustration. Maniacally it hurls itself at your throat, a pitted iron spike clenched in its fist.

Psi-ghoul:
COMBAT SKILL 20   ENDURANCE 30

Owing to your mastery of the psychic disciplines, add 2 points to your COMBAT SKILL for the duration of the fight.

If you win the combat, turn to **87**.

167

Your quick reactions, coupled with your Kai mastery, save you from being detected by the approaching cavalry. Using your skill, you calm your startled horse whilst simultaneously repelling the large but harmless savanna snake coiled about its foreleg. Minutes later the cavalry pass by, oblivious to your presence.

Turn to **213**.

168

An open wagon, drawn by a team of battle-scarred horses, hurtles along the street that borders the city wall. Standing beside the driver is a captain of the Senate House Guard. His thick black hair billows out behind him like the wings of an eagle as he calls desperately for reinforcements for the North Gate.

If you wish to answer his call by leaping on to his wagon, turn to **108**.

If you choose to ignore his call for help, turn to **286**.

169

Your horse rears up and leaps across the body of the dead Cave Leekhon, its senses ablaze with the choking rancid odour of the Leekhon's spilt blood. Banedon's steed follows close on your heels as you race through the tunnel, heedless of the many obstacles strewn in your path. Suddenly you emerge from the suffocating passage into the chill evening air: you have escaped. From the slopes of a wooded hill you stare down at a tiny village called Varta, perched on the edge of the Tahou flats.

The flats comprise fields of cultivated crops that form a fertile market garden two miles wide. They are farmed right up to the banks of the great moat that encircles the capital. Varta is deserted: its male inhabitants now shelter within the city walls, whilst the women and children have since travelled south to the safety of Navasari. As you ride through the empty village and descend on to the flats, you catch your first awe-inspiring view of the ancient city itself.

Turn to **100**.

170

As you step over the dead bodies and head towards the exit, the door crashes open and in rushes a squad of guards from the South Gatehouse, summoned by the owner of the hall. They are all armed with crossbows, which they aim at your chest. 'Yield, Northlanders!' orders their captain. 'You have no hope except our mercy.'

You cast your eyes around the hall for another exit but all are barred. Reluctantly you both raise your hands and are taken back to the South Gatehouse tower. Banedon, because he is a magician, is taken to another part of the city wall to be questioned, while you are imprisoned in a cell high in the tower itself.

Place an 'x' beside each of the Special Items, Backpack Items and Weapons listed on your *Action Chart* to indicate that they are no longer in your possession. Only if you rediscover them at a later stage of your adventure may you erase each 'x' and reuse them.

Turn to **134**.

171

Your arrow whistles across the hall and smashes harmlessly against the armour-hard skin of the nearest creature. Instantly their hissing ceases and they fix you with frightened stares. They cradle their leathery egg protectively in their webbed hands and slink down the stairs. You run to the top of the staircase and peer down into the gloom, but you can see nothing in the darkness.

If you have a Kalte Firesphere, a Lantern or a Torch and Tinderbox, turn to **33**.

If you have a Fireseed and wish to throw it into the hole, turn to **106**.

If you decide to unsheathe a hand weapon and descend the stairs into darkness, turn to **224**.

Using your weapon to avoid touching their evil-smelling bodies, you flick open the satchels slung over each of their shoulders. They are filled with all manner of items looted from the village. You tip the contents out and discover:

ENOUGH FOOD FOR 6 MEALS (Meals)
DAGGER (Weapons)
SWORD (Weapons)
SILVER CANDLESTICK
LANTERN
BRASS WHISTLE
BLANKET
SILVER GOBLET
SILK JACKET
TORCH
CRYSTAL DECANTER

Unless otherwise indicated, the articles are Backpack Items. If you wish to keep any, remember to make the necessary adjustments to your *Action Chart*.

You remount your horse and follow Banedon as he heads off along the track that leads out of the village.

Turn to **63**.

173

When you reach the bottom rung you are horrified to discover that the ladder stops short of solid ground: there is nothing but darkness below. You peer into the gloom but it is impossible to see how much further you have to descend. To your left you can see the faint outline of a ledge, but it is over twenty yards away.

If you have a Rope, turn to **7**.

If you wish to drop something in order to gauge the depth, turn to **261**.

If you wish to swing on the ladder and leap for the ledge, turn to **38**.

174

The soldiers in the crowded hall look at you with awe and grudging respect. They pride themselves on their fighting ability, but none can match your swift and skilful disposal of the Deldenians. You step over the bodies and head towards the door, but, before you reach it, it slams open and a squad of guards from the South Gatehouse rushes in, summoned by the owner of the hall. They are all armed with crossbows, and they aim them at your chest. Resistance would be suicidal and reluctantly you both raise your hands in surrender.

The guards escort you back to the South Gatehouse tower. Banedon, because he is a magician, is taken to another part of the city wall for interrogation, while you are imprisoned high in the tower itself.

Place an 'x' beside each of the Special Items, Backpack Items and Weapons that are listed on your *Action Chart* to indicate that they are no longer in your possession. Only if you rediscover them at a later stage of your adventure may you erase each 'x' and reuse them.

Turn to **134**.

175 — *Illustration X*

The climb to the arch at the top of the stairs is a slow and laborious one. Each step is as tall as a young tree, and the smooth, black stone offers few handholds. Several hours slip by before you reach the summit. There you stare down through the great archway at a stupendous sight.

The streets and buildings of an ancient civilization lie before you, disappearing into the gloom of a titanic chasm of immeasurable size. Ziggurats and towers, their carved walls cracked and crumbling, lean at impossible angles, having sunk into the soil over the centuries. This is Zaaryx, the legendary metropolis that was once home to a race fathered by Nyxator — the greatest of all dragons. It is the only city to have survived the Age of Chaos that followed the demise of their race.

A wide avenue leads from the archway to enter the city at a place flanked by two massive statues of dragons sitting on their haunches with their stone-fanged mouths agape. You stop to rest here and you must now eat a Meal or lose 3 ENDURANCE points.

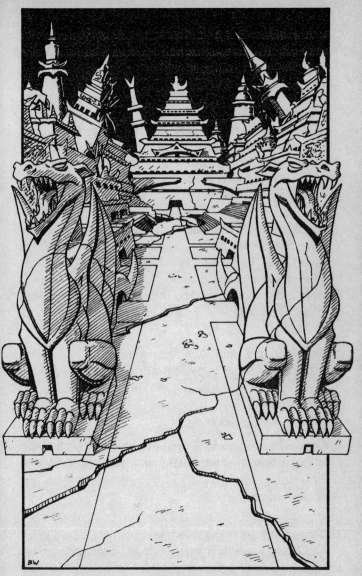

X.   Two massive statues of dragons flank the wide avenue
that leads from the archway to the city

You are about to set off into the city when you catch a glimpse of a shadowy figure moving furtively among the ruins of an edifice to your left.

If you have completed the Lore-circle of the Spirit, turn to **281**.

If you have yet to complete this Lore-circle, you can investigate the shadow; turn to **122**.

Or you can ignore it and continue along the avenue; turn to **61**.

176

'Follow me!' shouts Banedon, as he jumps his horse over the bodies of your slain attackers and gallops along the highway. He has survived the fight unscathed: by casting a magical net of sticky strands over a dozen rangers and their horses, he ensnared them all before they had a chance to level their lances at him.

The sergeant and the remnants of his company pursue you as you speed north along the highway. But you soon outdistance them and the sergeant orders off the chase, returning to the standing stones to free his netted men.

Only when he and his men are beyond the horizon do you rein in your horses and slacken the pace.

Turn to **213**.

177

You scoop the strongroom key from the guard's belt and hurry towards the gates while Sogh retrieves his silver. Once you are both safely inside the strongroom, you lock the heavy doors and begin to search for your equipment. The room is stacked to the ceiling with all manner of goods and articles that have been confiscated by the gatehouse guards. Contraband, stolen goods and illegal cargoes impounded at the South Gate are stored here before being either destroyed or sold at auction. It is rumoured that the gatehouse guards cream off the best booty for themselves, and it is no secret that the post of gatehouse commander is the most coveted of all in the Anarian army.

You discover all your Special and Backpack Items, but your Weapons are nowhere to be seen. However, there are several fine weapons lying on the shelves and you may rearm yourself with any of the following:

> SWORD
> AXE
> BOW
> QUIVER
> 6 ARROWS
> BROADSWORD
> WARHAMMER

Sogh is busily sifting through a mound of silver and antique jewellery, pocketing the choicest items and tossing aside the rest. He comes across a diamond and obsidian signet ring, and beams with delight. 'Ah! I knew it was here,' he says, and slips it inside his codpiece for safekeeping.

'Come, we've both got what we want; we'd best leave now before they discover the dead guards.' He beckons you to help him drag a table away from the wall and then proceeds to tap at the brickwork with the hilt of a dagger. Two minutes later he is becoming agitated, having tapped every brick over six square feet of wall without any result. You cast your eye over the surface and your Kai sense draws your attention to a brick in a different part of the wall. You tap it casually with the toe of your boot and a panel slides aside to reveal the secret passage.

'How did you . . . ' gasps Sogh, his eyes open wide with amazement.

'A lucky guess,' you reply, modestly, and enter the dark tunnel. Sogh follows and the panel slides closed just as a patrol of angry guards force open the strongroom door.

Erase the 'x' marks from your *Action Chart* to restore your rediscovered Special Items and Backpack Items, and remember to alter your Weapon list accordingly.

Turn to **197**.

178

'For one gifted in the ways of magic, you have a surprisingly poor sense of direction,' says the commander in a mocking voice. He signals to his men on to the parapet and you raise your hands in surrender; to resist would be suicidal.

Turn to **312**.

179

You reach the West Gate and climb the body-strewn stairs to the battlements. On this side of the city the mist is less dense and you can see regiments of Drakkarim warriors advancing in lines towards the great moat. Behind them are trundled huge machines of war designed to fire canisters of boiling oil and red-hot liquid metal over the city wall. Cavalry wait in reserve while siege towers and catapults are hauled forward by lumbering ghorkas and muscular leathery zull.

At the foot of the wall a unit of Salonese engineers are repairing the damage done to a bridge they constructed during the night. They have only one more plank to lay to make the bridge safe and enable a squad of Drakkarim assault-troopers to reach the West Gate. You see a soldier creep to the edge of the bridge and raise a large screen to protect the engineer who is laying this final plank.

If you have a bow and wish to use it, turn to **99**.

If you do not have a bow or do not wish to use it, turn to **249**.

180 – *Illustration XI (overleaf)*

With a bony fist she raps loudly on the door of the hut. Inside a croaky voice bids you enter and she tugs at your sleeve impatiently, urging you into the foul-smelling hovel. Seated on a threadbare carpet, and surrounded by what appear to be heaps of chicken bones, is a scrawny old man dressed completely in feathers. He has a long, pointed nose and a stubbly grey beard which grows to just below his beady bloodshot eyes. The crone kneels and whispers in his ear before bowing and leaving the hut. As the door swings shut the shaman scoops up a handful of bones, closes his eyes, and, with a sound like a flock of startled gulls, casts them in the air. After a full minute of chanting and waving his hands, the

XI. Seated on a threadbare carpet is a scrawny old man
dressed completely in feathers

old man opens his eyes and looks down on the bones which lie scattered on the beaten earth floor.

'You have many enemies, Northlander,' he says, his hook-like fingers tracing patterns around the bones, 'powerful enemies. They plot to prevent you from walking your chosen path, for that path will lead to their destruction. There is one who will tell you that he is a friend. You must not trust this one. There is treachery in his heart.'

The old man closes his eyes and lowers his head, as if he has fallen suddenly into a deep trance. You try to awaken him but he does not respond and eventually you decide to take your leave. You feel unsettled by the encounter, but when you return to Banedon you make light of the incident and suggest that you continue without further delay.

Turn to **52**.

181

Your pulse quickens as you look into the black abyss beyond the portal. You can make out no walls or roof, and the hollow wind that whistles in the darkness makes it easy to imagine that you are staring into a limitless void. There is a rope ladder fixed to the threshold of the portal: it descends into darkness below.

If you wish to gather up the ladder in order to judge how deep the abyss is, turn to **153**.

If you decide to descend the rope ladder, turn to **231**.

182

The net wraps itself around your legs and brings you down at the top of the stairs. You cannot prevent yourself from rolling forwards and, with a cry of fear and frustration, you tumble headlong down the hard stone staircase to land in a crumpled heap at the bottom: lose 3 ENDURANCE points.

Three soldiers are waiting for you. They clutch wooden staves in their sweaty palms with which they hope to beat you senseless. 'Get 'im!' they shout, and run forward to strike before you can disentangle yourself from the net.

Senate Guards: COMBAT SKILL 28   ENDURANCE 32

Because of your fall and your current entangled condition you cannot make use of a Weapon or Special Item during the first four rounds of combat. As you are unarmed, remember to reduce your COMBAT SKILL accordingly.

If you win the combat, turn to **90**.

183

You notch an arrow and let fly at a rider closing in on your left. The shaft pierces one of its eyes and lifts the loathsome creature out of its wolf-saddle, spinning him into the path of the following doom-wolves. His body brings down two of the ravening beasts and their riders, who are slammed into the ground as their mounts crash together in a tangled heap.

Your bow skill has bought you precious seconds in which to escape from the settlement. Banedon gallops past, his loose robe streaming out behind him like a pair of blue wings. You dig in your heels and urge your horse after him, with the shrill clangour of Giak war-cries ringing ever louder in your ears.

Turn to **293**.

184

With bow in hand, you crouch at the gap in the door and launch two arrows in as many seconds. The shafts strike home with deadly accuracy, piercing an eye of each reptilian and killing them instantly. As they fall, their crystal tube shatters and explodes with a tremendous, ear-splitting crack. The fragments burn fiercely and you are forced to cover your mouth with your cloak as you run, head down, through the billowing smoke and flames to a clearer section of the corridor beyond.

Turn to **241**.

185

At the end of the corridor a flight of steps leads down to an open prison door. Cautiously you peer around the doorway into the chamber beyond, where you see a man chained to the wall. He is lean and sinewy, with jet black hair and a moustache, which he has braided into his long sideburns in a style known as 'pirazin plaits', fashionable among Slovian men. He appears to be either asleep or unconscious.

You enter the chamber, moving swiftly and silently towards a staircase on the opposite side, and immediately he springs to life. 'Hold fast, Northlander,' he hisses. 'They'll catch y' for sure if you take the stairs. Let me loose and I'll show you a way to slip out o'here quicker than mist through a net.'

Quickly you consider his offer but choose to leave him, deciding instead to trust your Kai instincts to aid your escape. You shake your head and turn to leave, but the man is shrewd; he says something he knows will change your mind.

Turn to **316**.

186

The mouldering bones are encased in the tattered remains of a blue leather tunic and breeches. Both thigh bones are shattered and the skull and spine are cracked in several places, suggesting that this unfortunate man fell to his death from a great height. You can find no weapons, and the backpack and haversack that are strapped to his body are both unbuckled and empty, as if they have been looted. You check the corpse's right hand, but there are no rings on any of the bony fingers – this is not Maghana's son.

When you are satisfied that you have overlooked nothing, you leave the body and investigate the chamber.

Turn to **51**.

187

Gradually the track narrows, then disappears altogether, and you find yourselves riding through a sea of tall green wheat. You press on for over an hour until you see a faint glimmer of light stretching across the horizon in the far distance.

If you have the Magnakai Discipline of Huntmastery and have reached the rank of Principalin, turn to **140**.

If you do not possess this skill, or have yet to reach this Kai rank, turn to **74**.

188

The power of the ring greatly amplifies your psychic energies as you attack the Zakhan. They disrupt his control over the Orb of Death and enable you to penetrate his shield with an ordinary weapon.

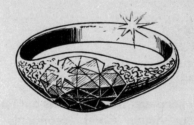

Zakhan Kimah: COMBAT SKILL 34   ENDURANCE 40

If you win the combat, turn to **350**.

189

You pull the hood of your cloak up to keep your face in shadow and stride boldly towards the two soldiers. 'I am in need of some information,' you say, disguising your Sommlending accent as best you can, 'and I'm sure you brave fellows can help me.'

'Maybe we can,' replies one soldier, stroking his beard and narrowing his eyes shrewdly, 'if the price be right.'

> If you wish to bribe these soldiers with Lune, turn to **253**.
>
> If you wish to bribe them with Gold Crowns, turn to **319**.
>
> If you wish to leave the barracks and walk back along Eastwall Lane, turn to **278**.
>
> If you prefer to continue on your way east, turn to **284**.

190

There is very little of use or value in this hut. You discover the following, all of which are Backpack Items:

> ROPE
> LANTERN
> BLANKET
> COMB

You may keep any of these items but remember to adjust your *Action Chart* accordingly. Banedon reminds you that it is rapidly getting darker, so you leave the hut and press on without further delay.

Turn to **123**.

191

You try to dodge aside but the mist whirls around you like a snake. An intense heat burns your body — it is as if you are surrounded by coils of white-hot metal — and your mind is filled with terrifying images of the supernatural: lose 6 ENDURANCE points.

Confident that it has ensnared another victim, the grey ghoul stalks forward. You fight to clear your mind of the swirling visions as the creature raises its hand and prepares to strike you down with a pitted iron spike.

Psi-ghoul:
COMBAT SKILL 20   ENDURANCE 30

Owing to the power of its psychic attack, you must reduce your COMBAT SKILL by 4 points for the duration of the fight.

If you win the combat, turn to **87**.

192

'Hold him tight, lads,' instructs the officer, as his men grab your cloak and tunic. 'They want this Northlander at the South Gate. Seems he's been making a nuisance of himself.'

They march you back along Eastwall Lane. Minutes later you reach the tower and the officer delivers you into the clutches of the angry gatehouse guard.

Turn to **162**.

193

Slowly the cavalry draws nearer; the faces of the soldiers are stern and unsmiling beneath the peaks of their winged helmets. Their leader, a sergeant, makes a signal and the horsemen change formation, drawing into a circle that quickly closes around you. 'State your business here!' bellows the sergeant. 'Why do you ride to Tahou?'

At first you are suspicious of their identity, but your basic Kai sixth sense tells you that these men are genuine Anarian rangers.

> If you wish to tell the sergeant the real reason you are riding to Tahou, turn to **279**.
> If you have an Invitation and wish to show it to him, turn to **136**.
> If you demand what right they have to hinder your passage to the capital, turn to **343**.

194

Your light flares into life, illuminating the rubbish-strewn passage. A moving shadow in the distance betrays the pickpocket, as he dives into a side entrance of a large, three-storey building.

> If you wish to follow him into the building turn to **217**.
> If you decide to let him escape, you walk back to Brooker Court and continue on your way; turn to **334**.

195

You throw out your hands to claw at the rope ladder but your fingers are numb with cold. You cannot close your grip and with a scream of anguish you slip and fall backwards into the black abyss. Your scream grows until you impact into a cold wet avenue of Zaaryx, 200 feet below.

Your life and your quest end here.

196

The guards look at you with distrust in their eyes.

They order you to dismount and one of them hurries off to fetch the gatehouse commander. Minutes later the officer strides into the enclosure, his face wearing the frown of a man who has gone without sleep for many nights. Wearily he casts his eye over you both. 'So you want to fight for Tahou, do you?' he says, sarcastically. 'How do I know you're not spies or saboteurs?'

If you possess the Magnakai Discipline of Invisibility, turn to **42**.

If you do not possess this skill, turn to **109**.

197

The passage is dark and very narrow and you are forced to turn sideways in order to move along it. To make matters worse the floor is littered with large rocks that graze and bruise your legs, making it difficult for you to stay on your feet.

If you have a Kalte Firesphere, a Lantern, or a Torch and Tinderbox, turn to **14**.

If you possess none of these items, turn to **327**.

198

Your shaft pierces the engineer's throat, sending him toppling into the moat. In panic, the soldier drops his screen and runs back across the bridge towards the Drakkarim. They view this as an act of cowardice and kill him out of hand as a warning to the Salonese.

Your bow skill has bought the defenders at the West Gate precious time to patch their battered defences. You are about to help them when a new threat looms to the north.

Turn to **249**

199

Your Magnakai Discipline of Divination screams a silent warning that the village harbours hostile enemies.

If you wish to investigate who these enemies might be, turn to **103**.

If you choose to heed your Kai sense and ride back into the wheatfields, turn to **111**.

200 — *Illustration XII*

You follow her along passages and sloping tunnels, down long flights of stairs and through magnificent chambers that no human eye has ever seen before. The alien splendour of this ancient city leaves you in awe of the race that once dwelt in these halls. For interminable hours you follow in her wake until you arrive at a circular chamber of rust-red stone. The floor descends in a series of wide steps that encircle the room, and in the middle of the tiers is a shallow pit with a stone dais at its centre.

At your approach, the dais glows with a crimson light that pulses like a living heart. Shimmering waves of silvery radiance sweep the steps and a chorus of voices, soft and sirenic, echo through the upper reaches of the chamber. You surrender yourself to instinct and step upon the dais, cupping your hands before you and raising your face to the roof. A golden light pours out of the darkness, soaking you in its brilliance and filling your senses with a glowing warmth. A gasp of awe arises from the tiers, now crowded with reptilians. They are the Crocaryx, the guardians of this city, the stewards of the Lorestone,

XII. At your approach, the dais glows with a crimson light and pulses like a living heart

who were placed here by the great God Kai. With joy and sorrow they have gathered to witness the fulfilment of their purpose, for your coming marks the end of their stewardship and the beginning of their demise.

High above you a shadow is taking form at the core of the golden light. It is dark and leathery and shaped like an egg. Slowly it breaks and peels open to reveal a sparkling crystal sphere: it is the Lorestone of Tahou, the object of your quest.

Turn to **150**.

201

Immediately you sense that the drunken soldier is not what he seems. He is a skilful pickpocket and he has just stolen one of your Special Items.

Pick a number from the *Random Number Table*. If the number you have chosen is *0–4*, the item stolen is the first one on your list of special items. If the number is *5–9*, he has stolen the second item on the list. If you possess only one Special Item, or no Special Items at all, then the pickpocket has stolen the first item on your list of Backpack Items.

If you wish to chase after him and try to retrieve your stolen item, turn to **62**.

If you choose to ignore the robbery and continue walking towards the square at the end of Brooker Court, turn to **334**.

202

Through the grille of the cell door you can see a great iron key, hanging from a hook on the wall a little way down the corridor. You focus your mastery of Nexus on this key and it rises slowly from the hook and glides towards your open hand. With a smile of triumph you grab the key, unlock the door, and step into the empty corridor.

Turn to **185**.

203

The mist coils around you like a python embracing its prey. Your body is engulfed by heat so intense that it seems as though you are surrounded by rings of white-hot metal, but your mind is filled with a stabbing icy pain. You lose 3 ENDURANCE points before your Psi-screen repels this psychic assault.

Turn to **301**.

204

Neither you nor the plains farmer are able to answer Khmar's riddle correctly, and you all forfeit your stakes (remember to delete what you wagered from your *Action Chart*). But Khmar is a very sporting fellow. He offers you the chance to win back what you have just lost by answering his next riddle correctly.

'This is Juno, my youngest boy,' he says, patting the head of his second son. 'I am four times as old as him now. Twenty years from now, I will be only twice as old as him. How old am I and how old is my son today?'

If you think you have both the answers to this riddle, add the two ages together and turn to the entry number that is the same as the total.
If you cannot answer the riddle, turn to **302**.

205

'There will be troops posted here at the Cauldron, ready day and night to pull you up when you are ready to leave Zaaryx,' says Senator Zilaris, as he helps you into the cradle that will lower you into the shaft. 'Just give the rope three stout tugs — that is the signal.'

Senator Chil appears to tell you everything is prepared for your descent. 'Good luck, Lone Wolf. I hope I will be here to welcome your safe and successful return, and that you will come to know me as a friend.'

The cradle rises and you are swung into position above the entrance. You stare down into the black abyss, your pulse quickening as a damp and icy wind whistles out of the shaft, carrying with it the cloying smell of decay.

With a wave, you signal your readiness and you are slowly lowered into the void.

Turn to **226**.

206

A minute passes before the lurker shows himself. He is a hunchbacked old man dressed in rags, with thin grey hair and a wrinkled face that bears the impressions of a lifetime's poverty. Two eyes, clouded with cataracts, stare up at you from the dark and dusty hole in the ground. 'Take what you will but please spare my worthless life,' he pleads.

'You have nothing to fear from me, old man,' you reply. 'Here, let me help you out of this hole.' And so saying you take hold of his scrawny arms and lift him with ease, for he weighs no more than a young child. He hobbles over to the fireplace and stirs the broth with a wooden spoon, which he keeps on a string around his neck. He offers you some of this smelly gruel but you refuse politely.

If you have a Meal in your Backpack and wish to offer it to the old man, turn to **271**.

If you do not have a Meal, or do not wish to give it to him, you leave the hut and continue, turn to **123**.

207

A sudden noise in the chamber behind distracts your attention from the door. From the depths of an archway comes the sound of something huge creeping towards you on clawed feet. Instinctively you reach for a weapon and brace your back against the door, but you shudder with horror when you see the creature that is approaching. A monstrous head protrudes from the darkness, as broad as the body of a horse, with jagged fangs that curve down over its lower jaw. Interlocking plates of horny scale cover its long neck and body, and coarse, feathery hairs fan out from the scarlet wattle below its throat. Its bulbous green eyes fix you with a hungry stare.

If you possess the Sommerswerd, turn to **336**.
If you do not possess this Special Item, turn to **67**.

208

With a casual wave of his hand, Chiban conjures up a quill and sheet of parchment. He begins to dictate the request for an audience and the quill moves of its own accord, as if guided by an invisible hand. The request, once completed, is then dispatched by messenger to the Anarium, the House of the Senate, where members of the governing council have gathered for an emergency assembly called for by the President himself. Within the hour the messenger returns with a scroll bearing the presidential seal.

'He has agreed to hear your plea, Lone Wolf,' says the aged magician, his ice-blue eyes scanning the official reply. Banedon congratulates you and you feel your spirits rise, but Chiban seems a little disappointed. 'I was expecting a private audience,' he says, 'but in view of the current situation, I suppose it is the best we can hope for. You must appear before the Senate this evening and state your reasons for wishing to enter the Tahou Cauldron. They will consider your request and vote accordingly. If they grant their approval, only you may enter. If they forbid you entry, you may not appeal against it. Their decision will be final.'

He hands you the scroll and arranges for his personal coach to take you to the Anarium. As you climb into the passenger seat, he and Banedon wish you good luck. 'I shall pray for your success,' says Chiban. 'And I shall pray that we are still alive to see your triumphant return, old friend,' says Banedon, as you exchange a farewell wave.

Turn to **300**.

209

Banedon rides alongside the crowded wagon and talks with Lortha as the procession continues on its way to Navasari. After a few minutes' conversation she hands him a scrap of parchment and they bid each other farewell.

'They are the last of the evacuees,' he says, as you continue your ride north. 'They expect the enemy to reach Tahou in two days' time. They've already seen Giak scouts and early this morning a squadron of Kraan were sighted high in the western skies. She advises us to steer clear of a village called Sidara. It's rumoured to have already fallen to the enemy. She also gave me this . . . '

Banedon hands you the scrap of parchment. It contains a few lines of Anarian script, an address and a signature. 'It's an invitation to stay at Chiban and Lortha's house in Tahou. It may be useful when we reach the city gate.'

Mark this Invitation on your *Action Chart* as a Special Item that you keep in your pocket. If you already carry the maximum number of Special Items, you must discard one in favour of this new item.

To continue your journey north, turn to **274**.

210

A surge of scarlet energy leaps from the orb and rips into your arm, hurling you backwards on to the ground (lose 5 ENDURANCE points). The Zakhan laughs mockingly as he raises the orb once more, this time to finish you for good. You are aware of the Zakhan's troops fighting a desperate battle at the West Gate and you know you must defeat him or else the city will be lost.

If you possess a Psychic Ring, turn to **188**.

(continued over)

If you possess the Dagger of Vashna, turn to **79**.

If you have neither of these Special Items, turn to **20**.

211

A cloud of arrows engulfs you and pain explodes throughout your body. You are mortally wounded, pierced by a dozen shafts, and although you fight to hang on to life it is a fight you cannot win.

Your life and your quest end here.

212

The cellar is full of rough-faced villains, laughing and bragging about their illegal exploits as they swill their sour ale. You cross the crowded floor and sit at the end of a table, as far away from the door as possible. A thin, wiry fellow with curly black hair approaches you with a tankard of foaming ale in one hand. You have taken his seat and he is determined to get it back.

If you have ever escaped from the South Gate tower, turn to **164**.

If not, turn to **315**.

213

It is late afternoon when you see the Tahou Hills. They appear like a mirage on the horizon, shimmering beyond the haze that rises from the sun-baked plain. Without stopping for food or rest, you hurry across the hot grasslands and follow the highway as it ascends towards the mouth of a pass. A stone watchtower guards the entrance to the hills and a cluster of whitewashed huts lie huddled around its base.

If you have the Magnakai Discipline of Pathsmanship and have reached the Kai rank of Tutelary, turn to **160**.

If you do not possess this skill, or have yet to reach this level of Kai training, turn to **314**.

214

You pull the ring from your pocket and focus your psychic abilities into its glowing yellow stone. The ring acts as an amplifier: it boosts your psychic energies and enables you to direct them against the monster that is now threatening to swallow you whole.

Zadragon: COMBAT SKILL 43   ENDURANCE 58

The power of the Psychic Ring increases your COMBAT SKILL by 8 points for the duration of the combat.

If you win the fight, turn to **93**.

215

With deadly accuracy you hurl the dagger at the shouting guard. He tries to duck but he is too close and cannot avoid being hit.

Pick a number from the *Random Number Table*. If you have the Magnakai Discipline of Weaponmastery with Dagger, add 4 to the number you have picked.

If your total is now 6 or less, turn to **287**.
If it is 7 or more, turn to **117**.

216

In the space of a few fleeting seconds you have loaded your bow and aimed it at the giant snake's head. With an angry hiss it darts its ugly head out of view. Almost immediately there is a tremendous noise as the snake rises into the air, propelled by a pair of powerful feathered wings. Two vulture-like forelimbs, tipped with sharp, rending claws, scrabble at the air as it streaks towards your chest.

Pick a number from the *Random Number Table*. If you have the Magnakai Discipline of Weaponmastery with Bow, add 3 to the number you have picked. If you have the Magnakai Discipline of Huntmastery, add 1.

If your total is now 0–7, turn to **9**.
If it is 8 or more, turn to **310**.

217

The moment you step into the building, the pickpocket lunges at you. He is wielding a cruel stiletto blade, which he attempts to sink into your chest.

Pickpocket: COMBAT SKILL 17   ENDURANCE 25

If you wish to evade combat and run back along the alley to Brooker Court, turn to **334**.
If you win the combat, turn to **155**.

218

Your spirits sink as you contemplate your fate, for the only way you know of escaping from this gigantic underground grotto has now been sealed off. However, you are not completely without hope, for your senses detect a powerful presence. It is a feeling you have known before when you have been close to discovering a Lorestone, but never has the sensation been as strong as it is here in this dark, subterranean world.

As your eyes become accustomed to the half-light, you look across the lake to see tiers of grey stone rising out of the water. They are the steps of a gigantic staircase, which ascends to an arch of rock veined with glittering minerals. You skirt the edge of the lake and arrive at the foot of these steps to discover a cave-like hollow chiselled from the stone.

You are exhausted and must now eat a Meal or lose 3 ENDURANCE points. Rather than attempt to go on, you climb into the empty hollow and settle down to sleep.

Turn to **97**.

219

Your light illuminates the tunnel ahead, and within a few minutes you have found your way through to a hillside exit that overlooks a tiny village called Varta, perched on the edge of the Tahou flats.

The flats comprise fields of cultivated crops that form a fertile market garden two miles wide. They are farmed right up to the banks of the great moat that encircles the capital. Varta is deserted; its male inhabitants now shelter within the city walls whilst the women and children have long since travelled south to the safety of Navasari. As you ride through the empty village and descend on to the flats, you catch your first awe-inspiring view of the ancient city itself.

Turn to **100**.

220 – *Illustration XIII*

You hurry down the stone stairs that lead to the West Gate arch. The gate has been holed by an explosive crystal and red-cloaked Drakkarim assault-troopers pour through the ragged gap. These evil warriors fight like fanatics, seemingly oblivious to any wounds they sustain. The gate guards are soon cut down and you are faced by three of these fearsome warriors. You must fight all three as one enemy.

Drakkar Assault-troopers:
COMBAT SKILL 30   ENDURANCE 42

Owing to their state of battle-frenzy, these enemies are immune to Mindblast (but not Psi-surge).

If you win the combat, turn to **30**.

221

Banedon once told you that Chiban lives in the city's North District. At the end of the alley you find a signpost that points the way north. You wait in the shadows until the coast is clear then hurry across the street into an avenue called Brooker Court.

Turn to **158**.

XIII. Red-cloaked Drakkarim assault-troopers pour through
the ragged gap in the gate

222

Cursing the delay, you steer your horse about and return along the narrow path of flattened corn that marks your route back to the highway. You have covered less than fifty yards when your horse rears up and shies away, refusing to go any further in this direction.

If you have the Magnakai Discipline of Animal Control and wish to use it, turn to **15**.

If you do not possess this skill, or do not wish to use it, turn to **296**.

223

Banedon casts a spell that fills the hall with a flash of light so intense that it stuns everyone for several seconds. In the confusion you are able to run out of the eating house and escape along the street.

Turn to **146**.

224

You can see nothing in the pitch dark. As you descend you run one hand along the smooth stone wall to keep your balance, and hold your weapon before you in the other, continually testing for obstructions.

If you possess the Magnakai Discipline of Pathmanship or Divination, turn to **133**.

If you do not possess either of these skills, turn to **264**.

225

Using the sole of your boot you push the bed across the trapdoor. The bedclothes are crawling with vermin and you are careful to avoid touching these tattered rags. Whoever is hiding below must know that the exit has now been blocked off, but still they remain silent.

If you now wish to search the hut, turn to **190**.
If you decide to leave the hut and continue, turn to **123**.

226

For the first few minutes of your descent you can see the red stone walls encircling the cradle. Then a jagged rim of rock marks the end of the shaft and you are plunged into total blackness. You can make out no walls or floor and the shaft itself is now just a small circle of grey in the darkness above.

If you have the Magnakai Discipline of Divination, turn to **251**.
If you do not possess this skill, turn to **53**.

227

You pace the cell like a caged lion, cursing your predicament and trying to think of a way to escape. After an hour you resign yourself to your fate and settle down on your haunches to sleep.

The prod of a spear haft wakes you from your slumber. 'On your feet,' snarls the brutish sergeant-at-arms, standing over you with his spear poised to strike again. Two soldiers grab you roughly by the collar and shove you through the open cell door into the arms of an escort that has come to take you before the Chief Magistrate. Your hands and feet are shackled with chains and you are bundled into a covered wagon waiting beside the South Gate. It moves off at breakneck speed, and by the time it reaches its destination, you are covered in bruises: lose 2 ENDURANCE points.

Turn to **142**.

228

The speed with which you slew your attacker strikes fear into the grisly hearts of the advancing ghouls. Slowly they slink away, their grey forms merging with the shadows at the far side of the lake. You are about to hurry away from the hollow, in case they should return with more of their kind, when you notice an odd-looking token lying next to the dead ghoul.

If you wish to examine the token, turn to **43**.
If you choose to ignore it and leave this place, turn to **175**.

229

The Giak enters the shadows just as you are ready to fire your bow. Although you can no longer see your target, you are able to sense approximately where he is.

Pick a number from the *Random Number Table*. If you have the Magnakai Discipline of Divination add 3 to the number you have picked.

If your total is now *0–5*, turn to **330**.
If it is *6* or more, turn to **107**.

230

You search the road ahead for somewhere soft to land, but the surface is strewn with sharp boulders.

Pick a number from the *Random Number Table*. If you have the Magnakai Discipline of Huntmastery, add 3 to the number you have picked.

If your total is now *0–6*, turn to **89**.
If it is 7 or more, turn to **297**.

231

The descent is slow and arduous and fraught with hazards. The wind becomes stronger and colder the further you go, numbing your fingers and sapping your strength. A sudden gust swings you into an outcrop of black rock, invisible in the gloom, and the impact forces you to lose your grip.

Pick a number from the *Random Number Table*. If you have the Magnakai Discipline of Huntmastery or Nexus, add 3 to the number you have picked.

If your total is now *0–1*, turn to **195**.
If it is *2–6*, turn to **332**.
If it is 7 or more, turn to **81**.

232

Reluctantly the lurker steps into the shaft of light that streams through the open hatch. A hunchbacked old man dressed in rags, he has thin, grey hair and a wrinkled face that bears the marks of a lifetime's poverty. Two eyes, clouded with cataracts, stare fearfully at you. You take hold of his scrawny arms and haul him out of the cellar with ease, for he weighs no more than a young child. You ask his name but he does not reply. Instead he hobbles around the hut, running his withered hands lightly over his meagre belongings and mumbling incoherently under his breath. He stops at the door and inclines his head towards you.

'Are you and your friend outside lost?' he asks in a thin and squeaky voice. 'I know a short cut to Tahou. Would you like me to show you?'

If you wish to take up the old man's offer of help, turn to **299**.

If you choose to decline his help, you leave the hut and continue; turn to **123**.

233

The circular walls shake violently and you slip and tumble headlong down the shaft, landing with a jolt on a slab of flat, spongy rock at the edge of a huge, subterranean lake. There is a tremendous roar as the ceiling of the tunnel collapses and tons of rock crash down to seal the shaft.

Turn to **218**.

234

The street leads to a far more grandiose part of the city. Government offices surround a broad plaza that narrows to a thoroughfare flanked by clean little town houses, each with a blossoming garden. You are wondering how such a prosperous avenue came to be named Gallows Street when you happen upon the Magistrates' Court.

Turn to **323**.

235

The beggars squabble noisily over who should have your donation and you are jostled on all sides as the bickering develops into an ugly brawl. Banedon grabs your cloak and pulls you clear as they set about each other tooth and nail.

'Generosity can sometimes be unwise in Anari,' he says, as you remount your white horses and ride away from the village. 'And costly too,' you reply, as you notice that your Backpack has been cut open. Unfortunately the beggars have stolen the items you have placed third and fourth on your list of Backpack Items. Erase these from your *Action Chart* before continuing your journey to Tahou.

Turn to **52**.

236

You flatten yourself against the floor and the net passes harmlessly over your head. Before the guard can react, you are back on your feet and running headlong down the stairs.

Three soldiers await you at the bottom of the staircase. They clutch wooden staves in their sweaty hands, ready to beat you senseless the moment you appear. 'Get 'im!' they shout, and run forward, clumsy and flat-footed compared with your cat-like strides. Before they can land a blow, you leap among them, striking left and right too quickly for their eyes to follow. They scream and clutch at their wounds as you make your getaway unharmed.

Turn to **90**.

237

By holding the mirror to the gap in the door you are able to see beyond it without exposing yourself. Your caution is well placed, for in the mirror you can see the reflection of two reptilians kneeling in the corridor beyond. Supported on their shoulders is a huge rod of crystal encircled with tubes and glowing metallic buttons.

If you have a bow and at least two arrows, turn to **184**.

If you do not, turn to **116**.

238

Your Kai mastery charges you with a superhuman response to this deadly situation. Suddenly the spinning arrows are approaching with exaggerated slowness, and every detail becomes crystal clear as they spiral lazily towards your heart. You raise your sword and strike the leading shaft, hacking it clean in two. Your backstoke shears through the underside of the second arrow, splintering it to useless matchwood. The archers stare in disbelief, their mouths agape. The sergeant and his men hesitate, frozen in awe of what they have just witnessed. Seconds slip away before they come to their senses and draw their swords.

'Take him!' yells the sergeant, and together they surge towards you. You cannot evade this combat, and because the corridor is narrow you must fight the guards two at a time.

Sergeant and Guard:
COMBAT SKILL 20 ENDURANCE 32
Tower Guards 3 and 4:
COMBAT SKILL 18 ENDURANCE 32
Tower Guards 5 and 6:
COMBAT SKILL 17 ENDURANCE 29

Your display of Kai mastery has made a big impression on Sogh, who fights by your side: add 2 to your COMBAT SKILL for the duration of the fight.

If you win, turn to **177**.

239

You have only one chance to kill the Zakhan before he releases another deadly bolt of energy from the Orb of Death.

Pick a number from the *Random Number Table*. If you have the Magnakai Discipline of Weaponmastery with Dagger, add 3 to the number you have picked. If you have completed the Lore-circle of Fire, add 1.

If your total is now 0–4, the dagger misses its target; turn to **20**.
If your total is 5 or more, it strikes the Zakhan in the heart; turn to **350**.

240

The dust cloud grows bigger and the rumble of hoofbeats can now be heard drifting towards you across the open plain. Twenty lightly armoured riders approach, their lances bearing blue pennants embroidered with the arms of Tahou, their faces stern and unsmiling beneath the peaks of their winged helmets. Their sergeant makes a signal and the horsemen change formation, drawing up into a circle that quickly closes around you. 'State your business here!' bellows the sergeant. 'Why do you ride to Tahou?'

At first you are suspicious of their identities but your basic Kai sixth sense confirms that these men are genuine Anarian rangers.

If you wish to tell the sergeant your real reason for riding to Tahou, turn to **279**.

If you possess an Invitation and wish to show it to him, turn to **136**.

If you demand to know what right they have to hinder your passage to the capital, turn to **343**.

241

You follow the corridor to a curved flight of alabaster stairs and descend them to a massive chamber. The floor is constructed of steely-blue metal flecked with silver and a hundred darkened archways line the walls. Directly ahead stand two gigantic doors of sheeted platinum, engraved with patterns breathtaking in their intricacy. The chamber is deserted, but as you cross the floor and approach the doors, you are acutely aware that any one of the arches could be hiding a legion of reptilians.

In the centre of the door there is a lock that consists of four hexagonal buttons, arranged in the shape of a pyramid, with one button at the top and three buttons in a line below it. Every time you touch a button a glowing number appears on its surface. Your basic Kai sense informs you that this is a combination lock; if you press each button several times until the correct numbers show on all four buttons the lock will release and the doors will open.

If you know the correct number to press for the top button, and the correct three-figure number for the bottom three buttons, add both numbers together and turn to the entry that has the same number as the total.

If you know only one of the two correct numbers that you need to open the lock, turn to the entry of that number.

If you do not know the correct numbers to press for either the top button, or the bottom three buttons, turn to **207**.

242

Leaving your horses and the South Gate tower behind, you enter a wide avenue flanked by workshops and houses, all built of red stone or rock sheathed in red plaster. The buildings themselves are small and densely packed, yet each one, no matter how humble, has a spire or tower that soars into the sky.

The large sleepy-eyed heads of stone dragons gaze down from the balconies of minarets, crowned either with bulbous, onion-shaped domes of copper, or with platforms housing engines of war recently installed.

Banedon points to an eating house and suggests that you stop there for some refreshment. Chiban's house is more than an hour's walk from here and you are ravenous after your long ride.

If you wish to enter the eating house, turn to **80**.
If you decide to ignore your rumbling stomach and continue your walk to Chiban's house, turn to **146**.

243 – *Illustration XIV*

Before you lies a huge chamber. Its walls are hung with silk and fine tapestries and its sunken floor is piled high with glittering treasures. As you enter, a perfumed breeze ruffles your hair and the sound of song-birds fills your ears.

Sogh leads you past a bubbling pool of crystal-clear water into an ante-chamber. Here, lying on a couch of vivid scarlet, rests the ruler of this sanctuary, dressed in an extravagant costume of many colours. His large, squarish face is framed by a hood trimmed with a strange purple fur. He stirs from his slumber and opens his coal-black eyes.

XIV. 'Kad-dul da-nar Li-ook!' he breathes, and a vivid
green flame engulfs the sparkling jewel

'Sogh! Who is this man?' he shouts, angrily. 'Why have you brought him here?' The thief tries to offer an explanation but it only serves to anger him even more. 'Sogh, you snivelling fool!' he bellows. 'You know it is forbidden to bring outsiders into the secret enclaves of the guild. I should have you flogged for your stupidity. For all we know, this Northlander could be a spy, or even . . . ' he pauses, staring up at you fearfully, 'an assassin.' He snatches a gem from his pocket and holds it in the air. 'Kad-dul da-nar Li-ook!' he breathes, and a vivid green flame engulfs the sparkling jewel.

If you have the Magnakai Discipline of Psi-shield, turn to **101**.

If you do not possess this skill, turn to **64**.

The doomwolves howl and their Giak riders cackle with glee as they hurl themselves upon you. You lash out at a grey-skinned rider, cleaving his grinning head in two, and swinging your arm back just in time to dispatch a doomwolf that is leaping towards your face. All around you the snarl and screech and press of bodies threaten to overwhelm your senses, but you are a Kai Master and in the heat of battle your nerve is ice cool. Grimly you fight with a speed and skill that leaves a dozen dead in as many blows. But you do not fight alone. Banedon rears into view, flashes of flame spurting from his fingers with a crack, like a whip, that echoes above the din of combat. Then another wave of wolf-riders appears. They charge into the fray, driving a wedge between you and your companion. A black sword cuts the air less than an inch from your scalp but you deal its wielder a fatal blow before he can strike a second time. He falls, yet his doomwolf mount leaps up and clings to your horse, its claws buried in the saddle leather, its foaming jaws snapping at your throat. You must dispatch this beast quickly before it drags you both to the ground.

Doomwolf: COMBAT SKILL 18   ENDURANCE 26

If you have the Magnakai Discipline of Animal Control, add 2 to your COMBAT SKILL for the duration of the fight.

> If you win and the fight lasts three rounds or less, turn to **306**.
> If you win and the fight lasts longer than three rounds, turn to **148**.

245

This tree-lined avenue leads to a large public garden called the Rainbow Park, so named because of the vast number of rare and colourful flowers that grow there. The park itself has been turned into an army encampment for those Anarians who have answered the President's desperate plea for defenders. Their banners, lit by the glow of a hundred camp fires, hang above the tents that cover the lush lawns. A couple of soldiers, armed with two-handed broadswords, which they rest across their shoulders, stand guard at the park gates.

> If you wish to ask them if they know where Chiban the Magician lives, turn to **17**.
> If you wish to continue along Rainbow Lane without stopping, turn to **288**.

246

With half your equipment discarded you are able to claw your way up through the black water. Finally you reach the surface, coughing and gasping for air. At first the incredible coldness stunned your senses, but now it revives them, spurring you to swim towards the distant shore that gleams faintly in the dim half-light.

Aching and numb to the bone, you heave yourself out of the lake and collapse on the flat, spongy rocks that line the shore.

If you have the Magnakai Discipline of Divination, turn to **298**.

If you do not possess this skill, turn to **41**.

247

You approach the twitching body of the dead sky-snake, your weapon held ready in case it should suddenly rear up and strike again. With grim fascination you inspect its venomous fangs and shiny green coils; you shudder when you think of how close you came to death.

Already a brace of plains vultures are circling overhead, waiting to feast on the creature's carcass. You mount your horse and follow Banedon as he retraces the route back to the highway. You are now hungry and must eat a Meal or lose 3 ENDURANCE points.

To continue, turn to **318**.

248

Crouching in the shadows beneath the staircase, you look to the end of a torchlit corridor, where a soldier stands guard at a pair of solid iron gates. 'Your weapons and equipment are on the other side of that gate, my friend,' whispers Sogh. 'It's the tower strongroom, although it's not as strong as they'd like to think. They caught me inside once, but they never found out how I managed to get in. There's a secret passage that leads through the wall to the stables outside. If we can get past that guard and into the strongroom, you can get your equipment back, I can get what I came here for, and we can both get out through the stables.'

'But what about my friend?' you reply, worried about Banedon's safety.

'He's not here. I overheard the guards say they were taking him to the Eastgate Barracks. I'd worry about his neck after you've saved your own if I were you.'

You stare at the guard, a plan slowly forming in your mind. 'Give me that purse of silver,' you say, holding out your hand.

'Now, wait a minute, I . . .' replies Sogh, in a fluster.

'Don't argue,' you retort. 'You'll get it back. I just need the right sort of bait to hook us this fish.'

Reluctantly he hands over the purse. Silently you leave the shadows and creep along the corridor, taking care to avoid the pools of flickering torchlight. When you are within ten feet of the guard, you begin to lay a trail of silver Lune all the way back to the staircase. The guard notices the glint of silver and cannot resist the temptation; he leaves his post to collect the coins. You wait tensely, sword in hand, as he approaches slowly. He is within a few feet of your hiding place when suddenly he sees you and begins to shout for help.

You must act quickly or his cries will summon every guard in the tower.

> If you have the Magnakai Discipline of Psi-surge and have reached the rank of Principalin, turn to **84**.
> If you wish to attack him with your sword, turn to **3**.
> If you wish to throw your dagger at him, turn to **215**.

Further along the battlements a group of determined Giak soldiers have climbed the wall, using a scaling ladder. Leading their attack is a large scaly Gourgaz, who wields a two-handed axe with devastating effect. It cuts a gruesome path through the Anarian defenders and launches itself at you.

Gourgaz: COMBAT SKILL 23   ENDURANCE 34

This creature is immune to Mindblast (but not Psi-surge).

If you win the combat, turn to **303**.

250

You walk along the narrow, cobblestoned street, taking care to avoid passing too close to windows and doorways, where the glare of firelight is brightest. The city is in a sullen mood. With their women and children safe in the south, the soldiers and citizens busy themselves with preparations for the battle that is imminent. Heavy steps and the clank of weapons echo along the street as a troop of Slovian mercenaries march by, with scarlet- and black-striped shields on their arms, and polished halberds resting on their mailed shoulders. You follow as they march towards a building in the distance, where their officer orders them to halt and fall out. Most of the soldiers then enter the building, but two remain outside to talk and share a pipe of Lourden tobacco. A sign fixed to the building says:

EASTGATE BARRACKS

If you wish to question the mercenaries about Banedon, turn to **189**.

If you wish to try to enter the barracks unnoticed, turn to **68**.

(continued over)

If you decide to continue walking along Eastwall Lane, turn to **284**.

251

Deprived of your sight, as you descend into the stygian void, your Kai perception compensates by becoming more sensitive and more acute. An image forms in your mind of the events taking place around the Cauldron. You see the winch and the faces of the Senate guards, who are feeding the rope that supports your cradle. They are joined by another, who has come to help with their task. He takes his place at the lip of the shaft and grips the rope, but hidden in his hand is a razor-sharp blade! Your throat tightens with fear as you picture the gloating face of Senator Chil.

Turn to **53**.

252

Like most southern Anarian peasants, these farm hands are simple folk. They have heard nothing of the war in the north, and know nothing about the Darklord armies that are poised to assault their capital. All they are able to tell you is that a great many wagons carrying 'Takas', or rich city folk, have travelled the road to Navasari in the last ten days.

They would be happy to share their humble meal of corn soup with you, but the smell of their dung fire has destroyed your appetite and you refuse their offer politely. Banedon, who has been talking with the owner of the house, returns to his horse and nods at the signpost. 'It's pointing the wrong way. A few days ago one of the Takas' wagons ran into it and nobody has bothered to fix it yet.'

With a wave, the farm hands bid you farewell as you urge your horses back on to the highway. You are now hungry and must eat a Meal or lose 3 ENDURANCE points.

Turn to **318**.

253

The mercenaries demand ten Lune in advance before they even hear your question.

If you have this sum, and wish to pay it, do so and turn to **19**.

If you do not have ten Lune, or do not wish to pay them this amount, you either try to enter the barracks unseen; turn to **68**.

Or, leave the barracks and walk back along Eastgate Lane; turn to **278**.

254

The ghouls clamber up the rocky base of the steps and hurl themselves into the hollow with fanatical zeal. They are all unarmed, but their claw-tipped fingers are as sharp and as deadly as knives.

Ghoul Pack: COMBAT SKILL 24   ENDURANCE 35

If you win the combat, turn to **147**.

255

The commander narrows his eyes. 'Bah!' he snorts. 'Let 'em enter. We need all the men we can get. Their blood's as good as any that'll be spilled in the defence of this city.'

You cast a glance at Banedon and smile as he wipes a bead of sweat from his brow.

Turn to **113**.

256

'I seek the Lorestone of Tahou,' you reply, boldly. 'I am the Kai Lord, Lone Wolf, and I quest for the wisdom of Nyxator, that I may vanquish the spawn of his enemies and save my people from destruction.'

Her harsh gaze softens, as your proud words fill the chamber with resonant echoes. You sense a sadness within her, but she replies with words of joy that form in your mind. 'Your quest will be fulfilled, as it was by your sire many centuries ago. We have waited long for your coming, Skarn, and we will fulfil our duty to He who gave us life.'

She opens the great platinum doors and beckons you to follow her.

Turn to **200**.

257

The highway twists like a restless snake as you gallop headlong through the darkening Tahou Hills. The unholy baying of the doomwolves draws steadily closer as you fight desperately to keep your tired horses ahead of the ravening pack. Three miles from the watchtower settlement, the fastest pack members draw level with you as you race along a dry watercourse. Their eyes and fangs glint evilly in the moonlight as they cut across your path, forcing you to stand and fight.

Turn to **244**.

258 – *Illustration XV (overleaf)*

Relentlessly the enemy pour their fire upon the north and west city walls, until the black sky above Tahou takes on a vivid scarlet glow. The defenders look to their weapons uneasily and pray that the gods are with them, at least until dawn. And when the first rays of dawn light show above the eastern hills, no mists enshroud the armies of Darklord Gnaag – they are massed in all their glory, awaiting the order to attack. You cast your eye across this sea of doom and mark the many regiments of evil that are ranged against the walls of Tahou.

The armoured legions of Vassagonia are the first to advance, moving in ordered columns towards the West Gate. At their head walks a figure sheathed in gold around whom a cold blue fire glows intensely. He strides within range of the city archers and they send a cloud of arrows to greet him, but these shatter and crackle when they encounter his impregnable glowing shield. He crosses the siege bridge and halts before the West Gate. In his hand is an orb of black metal. He holds it before him and mouths an incantation. Instantly a bolt of scarlet flame lances from the orb, destroying the great doors with a thunderous boom. Proudly he strides into the city and the defenders melt before him. One summons enough courage to attack him with a spear. There is a crackling flash and in an instant the soldier is transformed into a pile of glowing ash.

XV. A Defender attacks him, driving his spear through the
cold blue flames

He advances unchecked and undaunted by all attacks, for they cannot penetrate his magical shield. Only when he comes face to face with you does he stop.

'I have come for you, Lone Wolf,' he says, a cruel smile on his lips. You gaze into the ice-cold eyes of Zakhan Kimah, ruler of Vassagonia. As he raises his orb of black metal, you steel yourself for the battle that is about to commence.

If you have the Sommerswerd, turn to **48**.

If you do not possess this Special Item, turn to **210**.

259

Sogh looks at you sheepishly as you search the dead guards. 'I'm no fighter,' he says, apologizing for his cowardly behaviour. 'I've no stomach for it.' He grimaces at the sight of the bloodstained bodies but manages to overcome his squeamishness when he spies a gold ring and a full purse on one of them.

Your search reveals four useful items:

> 2 SWORDS
> 1 DAGGER
> 1 IRON KEY

You let Sogh keep the ring and the purse, and hand him one of the swords, which he is reluctant to accept. The other three items you keep (mark them on your *Action Chart*).

After hiding the bodies, you follow Sogh as he leads you through the chambers and corridors of the South Gatehouse tower. Twice you are almost discovered but your Kai skills, and Sogh's thief-like agility, save you both from further confrontation until you reach the ground floor of the tower.

Turn to **248**.

260

In a split second you counter his attack with a savage swipe that shears his arm off at the elbow. Arm and dagger fall to the table and the soldier collapses screaming to the floor. His comrade kicks back his bench and steps away as he fumbles for his sword. With a drunken yell he unsheathes the blade and leaps forward in a reckless attack.

Drunken Mercenary:
COMBAT SKILL 15   ENDURANCE 26

If you wish to evade combat, turn to **328**.
If you stay and win the combat, turn to **170**.

261

You may drop either a coin (a Gold Crown or a Lune), a Special Item, a Backpack Item, or a Weapon. When you have decided which of your possessions you are willing to risk, erase it from your *Action Chart*.

Turn to **280**.

262

Your psychic Kai sense warns you of imminent danger if you take the track to the left.

If you wish to investigate the danger, turn to **45**.
If you choose to heed your Kai sense and take the track to the right, turn to **63**.

263

Your skin prickles when you see the old man mouth your name, for his words sound in your head as if he were standing next to you and whispering them in your ear. 'Come hither, Lone Wolf,' he breathes. 'Your purpose here is known to me. I, Gwynian of Varetta, will aid your quest.'

Your immediate reaction is to turn and flee, but your Kai senses reveal that this man speaks the truth; he can help you find the Lorestone of Tahou.

Drawn by his command and your own curiosity, you climb the steps of the Magistrates' Court and follow him into his private chambers. There he explains how he has learned of your identity and purpose.

Turn to **76**.

264

In the pitch blackness you fail to see a false section of the stair which conceals a shallow hole. As you tread on the false step, it collapses, and your foot sinks into the hole to become ensnared among a mass of hooks. Their barbed tips hold you trapped, for you dare not withdraw your foot quickly in case you rip your leg to shreads: lose 3 ENDURANCE points.

Turn to **307**.

265

Including the broth, which smells awful, there is very little of use or value in the hut. You discover the following articles, all of which are Backpack Items:

> COMB
> ROPE
> LANTERN
> BLANKET

You may keep any or all of these items but remember to adjust your *Action Chart* accordingly. You are about to leave when you notice a trapdoor set into the floor near the fireplace.

If you wish to open the trapdoor, turn to **154**.
If you choose to ignore it and continue your trek to Tahou, turn to **123**.

266

You raise your hood and wrap yourself in your Kai cloak to minimize the risk of being cut by broken glass. Leaping feet first, you escape through the window with only a few minor scratches (lose 1 ENDURANCE point), but the glass shatters with such a terrific crash that it alerts the soldiers on guard at the side door. They surround the carriage and arrest the driver, forcing you to abandon your hopes of escaping that way.

Turn to **39**.

267

The sergeant-at-arms orders his men to surround and disarm you both. Sogh immediately drops to his knees and begs for mercy; he blames you for everything, saying that you released him and forced him to accompany you against his will. 'Silence, weevil! You'll get your chance to tell your tale to the Chief Magistrate. Maybe he'll believe you . . . ' growls the sergeant before casting an angry glance at the dead soldier, 'and maybe he won't.'

You are led back to your cell and four burly armed guards are placed outside the door with orders to shoot to kill if you should attempt another escape.

Turn to **227**.

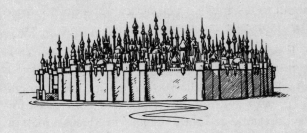

268

Guyuk is a nervous and jittery sort of man. He is afflicted with all manner of tics and twitches and is given to worrying about anything and everything. Recently his condition has worsened and in light of events in the north it is not difficult to understand why.

'Oh! What's to become of us? Where will it all end?' he mutters, wringing his pudgy hands and casting his eyes to the rafters. 'Every day for the last two weeks wagons filled with women and children have been leaving Tahou for the south, yet the Senate tell us that nothing is wrong, that we should go about our business and not concern ourselves with city affairs. Well, I for one am not fooled. I tell you they're keeping us in the dark about what's really happening and I'm not going to wait around to suffer the consequences. I'm closing up and moving out at the end of the week, and if you two gentlemen would take some friendly advice, you'd be wise to do the same.'

Someone in the tavern is calling for more lovka. Before you can question Guyuk further, he snatches up a bottle and scurries away to serve his thirsty customer.

If you now wish to order some food, turn to **88**.
If you decide to retire to your room, turn to **156**.

269

When you have finished your meal you talk at length about your journey from Dessi and your quest for the Lorestone of Tahou. Chiban produces a map of the city, which he unfurls on the floor of his study, the only surface not cluttered with magical equipment. With his toe he points to the location of the Tahou Cauldron: it is in the Square of the Dragons in the West District of the city.

'The Cauldron is a tunnel-shaped hollow with a circular shaft at its base. The shaft descends to the ruins of the ancient city of Zaaryx, 500 feet below the streets of Tahou. Legend tells us that the Lorestone was thrown into the Cauldron to prevent the Black Zakhan of Vassagonia from capturing it during the Great Khordaim War. The shaft was closed off and has remained sealed for the past 360 years.' He looks up from the map and you notice that his smiling features are now sad and composed.

'At dawn the armies of Darklord Gnaag will be at the gates of the city and the battle of Tahou will have begun. My duty is here, in the defence of my beloved city, otherwise I would willingly accompany you on your search. There is only one man who can help you now, for he is the only one that can grant you access to the shaft that descends to Zaaryx. He is President Toltuda of Anari. Come, I will arrange an audience with him immediately.'

Turn to **208**.

270

You rise and run along the battlements, escaping death by inches as the stone ball shears away the parapet and walkway where you were sheltering. 100 yards further on a tower looms into view; it is one of many that reinforce the city wall. You can hardly believe your eyes when you notice that your companion Banedon, is standing behind the crenellations. You wave and shout to him but the noise of battle drowns your call.

Turn to **131**.

271

Gratefully he accepts your offer and adds the food to the broth bubbling on the grate. He tells you that he is a hermit and has lived here, at the edge of the gorge, for most of his life. He is nearly blind but he knows every inch of these hills as well as he knows his own hut, and he offers to show you and Banedon a short cut to Tahou.

If you wish to accept his help, turn to **37**.

(continued over)

If you choose not to accept his help, you leave the hut and continue, turn to **123**.

272

You have a strong premonition that death will befall you if you stay on board the wagon.

If you wish to heed your Kai sense and leap from the speeding wagon, turn to **230**.

If you decide to ignore your premonition and stay on board, turn to **340**.

273

You are about to enter the square at the end of Brooker Court when you suddenly realize that you have been robbed. The drunken soldier was not drunk at all: he was a skilful pickpocket.

Erase the second Special Item on the list on your *Action Chart*. If you only have one Special Item, you must delete this. If you have no Special Items at all, delete the first Backpack Item noted on your *Action Chart*.

If you wish to run back to the tavern alley and chase after the pickpocket, turn to **94**.

If you choose to let him go and continue on your way, turn to **334**.

274

For three hours you ride without pause or rest along the Tahou highway. On either side the whispering grasses of the Anari plain stir lazily in the thin breeze of morning. Villages are few, but wherever there are trees you are sure to find a group of huts nearby.

The highway descends along a ridge towards a copse of stunted trees, where a circle of simple dwellings have been built around a well. At your approach a bell is sounded and several peasants appear, each holding a basket of assorted wares, which they urge you to buy.

If you wish to examine these wares, turn to **331**.
If you wish to continue through the village without stopping, turn to **52**.

275

Maghana leads you to another room, one of several that lead from his sumptuous chamber, and approaches a dais standing near the door. He passes his hand over a crystal set into its surface and at once a section of the wall moves inwards, exposing darkness beyond. An icy damp wind fills the room, carrying with it a cloying smell of decay. Elsewhere in the chamber are tables laden with equipment, placed here, no doubt, for those who dare venture beyond the windswept portal.

276–277

'Take what you need,' says Maghana, his voice barely audible above the howl of the wind, 'then go.' He ushers Sogh from the chamber and locks the door behind him.

If you wish to examine the equipment, turn to **13**.
If you choose to ignore the equipment and investigate the portal instead, turn to **181**.

276

The impact of your killing blow knocks the guard headlong backwards on to the hard stone floor. Unfortunately, the noise of combat has alerted his comrades and, as you stoop to grab the key from the dead man's belt, you hear the sound of their hob-nailed boots as they storm down the stairs. The leading pair are armed with bows and, as they reach the bottom of the staircase, they kneel and take aim.

'Surrender or die!' shouts their sergeant-at-arms, brandishing an axe.

If you wish to raise your hands in surrender, turn to **267**.
If you wish to defy his order, turn to **95**.

277

The dragon-like eyes of the monster blaze with hatred and a deep growl rumbles from its fanged maw as it makes ready to attack.

Zadragon: COMBAT SKILL 43   ENDURANCE 58

This creature is immune to Mindblast (but not Psi-surge).

If you win the combat, turn to **93**.

278

You have not gone far when, to your horror, you find yourself standing in front of the South Gate tower. The guards recognize you immediately and raise the alarm. You turn to run but a troop of cavalry surges out of the gatehouse and you are quickly surrounded.

If you wish to stand and fight these soldiers, turn to **44**.

If you choose to surrender to them, turn to **162**.

279

'Seems we have a pair of travelling clowns come to entertain us with fairy stories,' sneers the sergeant, while his men laugh disdainfully at your explanation. He draws his curved cavalry sword and points the blade menacingly towards your chest; his men cease their sniggering. 'You're both under arrest on suspicion of spying. Drop your weapons – at once!'

If you wish to obey the sergeant's order, turn to **24**.
If you wish to resist arrest, turn to **85**.

280

It takes a little over three seconds for the object to hit solid ground, and you judge the drop to be at least thirty feet – too far to jump safely. Rather than risk your legs, and possibly your life, on such a jump, you decide to try to reach the ledge.

Turn to **38**.

281

You sense an aura of psychic energy burning fiercely at the core of the moving shadow. The creature possesses a supernatural force of great destructive power. To approach it could be fatal, yet to ignore it could prove equally disastrous.

If you wish to raise your Psi-screen and approach the shadow, turn to **166**.

If you choose to avoid it by hurrying away, turn to **61**.

282

The roof of the cave and the tunnel beyond is high enough for you to ride through it on horseback. But the interior is pitch black, and if you are not to stray off course, you will need some form of light to illuminate the way ahead.

If you possess a Kalte Firesphere, a Lantern, or a Torch and Tinderbox, turn to **219**.

If you do not possess any of these items, turn to **341**.

283

The metal is cream-coloured and wafer thin, and the design embossed on the surface appears to be an intricate mathematical equation. You apply your mind to solving the numerical riddle and are close to an answer when suddenly the metal bursts into flames. You fling the flaring token away instantly but your hand is still badly burned by the flash — lose 4 ENDURANCE points

You curse the device but console yourself with having solved the riddle: the answer is 320. (Make a note of this number in the margin of your *Action Chart*; it may prove useful at a later stage of your adventure.)

Turn to **130**.

284

You continue along the street as it follows the curve of the city wall. To your left you notice a tavern with its door and windows boarded up. Just beyond it a street branches off to the left. A rusty iron sign reads:

GALLOWS STREET

If you wish to enter Gallows Street, turn to **234**.
If you wish to continue along Eastwall Lane, turn to **55**.

285

The Giaks fix you with steely stares, their yellow eyes open wide with shock as they fumble for their weapons. However, before they are able to unsheathe their swords and scramble to their feet, you leap forward and attack.

Giak Scouts:
COMBAT SKILL 15   ENDURANCE 20

Owing to the surprise of your attack, ignore any ENDURANCE losses you sustain in the first two rounds of combat.

If you win the combat, turn to **21**.

286 – *Illustration XVI (overleaf)*

The enemy begin bombarding the wall with huge stone balls fired from catapults that they have wheeled to the edge of the great moat. The first of these missiles drop from the sky without warning to tear vast holes in the parapets and walkways. Immediately you take cover but are horrified to see one of these huge missiles hurtling directly towards you.

XVI.   The enemy begin bombarding the wall with huge
stone balls fired from catapults

Pick a number from the *Random Number Table*. If you have completed the Lore-circle of Solaris add 4 to the number you have picked.

If your total is now *0–5*, turn to **112**.
If it is *6* or more, turn to **270**.

287

The dagger sinks deeply into his chest, knocking him to the ground. He screams at the sudden pain and his cry alerts a patrol of guards on the floor above. You leave your hiding place and run towards the dying soldier, your hand outstretched to snatch the strongroom key from his belt. But before you reach the man you hear the hobnailed boots of the patrol storming down the stairs behind. The leading pair are armed with bows, and as they reach the bottom of the staircase, they kneel and take aim. 'Surrender or die!' shouts their sergeant-at-arms.

If you wish to raise your hands in surrender, turn to **267**.
If you choose to defy his order, turn to **95**.

288

The lane skirts the edge of Rainbow Park as it heads towards the guildhalls and emporiums of the city's West District. As you approach the Guildhall of Armourers, a patrol of guards, led by an officer wearing the crest of the Tahou garrison, suddenly appears from a side street and comes marching towards you. As soon as the officer catches sight of you he orders his men to halt and load their bows. 'Stop!' he commands. 'Stop at once or we'll open fire!'

If you wish to surrender to this patrol, turn to **344**.
If you wish to ignore the officer's command and turn and run, turn to **211**.

289

The icy water clogs your nose and throat and numbs you to the bone. Desperately you fight to control the panic gnawing at your insides as your air-starved lungs fill your chest with an agonizing pain.

If you have a Vial of Blue Pills, turn to **25**.
If you do not possess this item, turn to **329**.

290

The leader of the approaching cavalry, a sergeant, signals to his men to change formation. They leave the highway and draw up in a circle, closing around your hiding place. The sergeant unsheathes his curved cavalry sword, holds it at arm's length, and edges his mount nearer so that the blade hovers menacingly just before your chest. 'You're both under arrest!' he bellows, 'on suspicion of spying. Drop your weapons at once!'

If you wish to obey the sergeant's order, turn to **24**.
If you choose to resist arrest, turn to **85**.

291

The deluge engulfs you so quickly that it is impossible to avoid inhaling the fine grit. As you do so, a terrible pain stabs at your chest: the dust contains the spores of a deadly fungus that is now poisoning your lungs. Unless you have the Magnakai Discipline of Curing, and have reached the Kai rank of Tutelary or higher, you must lose 8 ENDURANCE points.

If you are still alive, turn to **233**.

292

The men are plainly displeased that you have interrupted their conversation. One of them, a sallow-faced knave with dark eyes and curly black hair, snatches a jug from the table and takes a long swig. He slams it down and turns to his friend.

'Did you know,' he says, red wine squirting through his rotted teeth, 'my brother Ghane was killed in Ragadorn last year? He was stabbed in the back by a lousy Northlander.' Slowly he turns his head and stares coldly into your eyes. 'I hate Northlanders,' he snarls. 'They're all cowardly, backstabbing scum!' You notice his hand leave the jug and slip below the table.

If you wish to tell him you are sorry to hear what happened to his brother, turn to **8**.

If you wish to prepare for combat in case he attacks you, turn to **86**.

If you decide it would be wise to leave the eating house, turn to **347**.

293

The wolf-riders give chase but their pursuit is half-hearted and you have covered less than a mile when you hear the Giaks call off their hunt. They console themselves by hurling threats and vile curses at your backs as you disappear swiftly into the dusk.

The highway emerges from the hills at a village called Vanta, situated on the edge of the Tahou flats. The flats consist of fields of cultivated crops forming a fertile market garden two miles wide which is farmed right up to the banks of the great moat that encircles the capital. Vanta is deserted: its male inhabitants now shelter within the city walls, whilst the women and children have travelled south to the safety of Navasari. As you leave the empty town and descend on to the flats, you catch your first awe-inspiring glimpse of the ancient city.

Turn to **100**.

294

You shake your head in disbelief when you see who is sitting in the Chief Magistrate's chair. It is Gwynian, the Sage of Varetta, the man who foretold the dangers of the Chasm of Doom and helped you find the Lorestone of Varetta.

'Our stars unite, Lone Wolf,' he says, the trace of a smile wrinkling his kindly face. 'Destiny has decreed that we should meet again.'

Turn to **54**.

295

You grip the sun-sword in both hands and strike out at the bolt as it surges towards your chest. There is a terrific jolt and a splash of white sparks as the sword deflects the bolt, sending it screeching back along the corridor. It explodes among the reptilians with an ear-splitting crack, destroying them and their weapon and scattering their burning remains all over the walls and floor. You cover your face with your cloak and run, head down, through the billowing smoke and flames to a clearer section of the corridor beyond.

Turn to **241**.

296

Suddenly a tremendous noise fills your ears as a huge snake rises above the crops ahead, propelled into the air by a pair of powerful feathered wings. Two vulture-like forelimbs, tipped with sharp rending claws, scrabble the air as it dives towards your chest.

Turn to **82**.

297

You dive, roll twice, and bounce to your feet, suffering nothing more serious than a scratched shoulder and a bruised knee: lose 1 ENDURANCE point.

To enter the tower, turn to **131**.

298

Gradually, as the feeling returns to your frozen limbs and your heart ceases to hammer in your chest, you feel bitterness and resentment welling up inside. You lift your face and give vent to an angry shout, cursing Senator Chil for his act of callous treachery that so nearly sealed your doom. Your voice travels through the dark towards a tiny speck that is the shaft of the Cauldron, 500 feet above, but none hear your cry. The Senate is convinced that you have perished in the fall and have ordered the plug to be lowered back into position. Helplessly you stare into the void and watch, with fear and frustration, as the tiny speck flickers and then disappears.

Turn to **218**.

299

You follow the old hermit back into the gorge and along the dry watercourse. He leads you to a cave, its entrance partially hidden by a rockfall. 'Enter and follow the tunnel through the hillside and you will soon arrive at a place close to the capital.' Before you can thank him he turns and hobbles away, eager to return to the warmth of his hut.

Turn to **31**.

300 – *Illustration XVII*

The great flagstoned precinct at the entrance to the Anarium is packed with hundreds of people. Senate officials, soldiers and citizens crowd the steps that give access to the grand foyer and outer chambers of the hall. You notice that a side entrance is being used exclusively by army scouts who arrive with dispatches and leave with orders for the lookouts hidden in the surrounding hills. You take a calculated gamble and order the carriage driver to draw up at the side entrance. This bold move pays off; upon seeing your presidential scroll not only do the guards allow you into the Anarium, but you are escorted to the Appellant's Gallery inside the assembly hall itself.

From your seat in the gallery you stare down at an oval hall, ringed by twelve arches beneath which the senators of Anari sit upon their throne-like chairs of lacquered oak. President Toltuda occupies a seat in the centre of the hall and presides over a heated discussion that is raging back and forth. Having heard all sides of the argument he calls for a vote, and the issue is decided by a show of hands.

XVII.   President Toltuda occupies a seat in the centre of the
hall and presides over a heated discussion

'We now come to a quite extraordinary matter, which has been raised by one of our most eminent citizens,' says President Toltuda, introducing your appeal to the Senate. He turns to the gallery and calls out, 'Sommlending Lord, Lone Wolf, please make yourself known to the assembly.'

You rise from your seat and bow to the senators. 'Please present your request to us, Lone Wolf,' says the President, and a hush descends on the hall as you explain the purpose of your journey to Tahou. When you have finished the President calls upon the senators to speak.

'I say we should help the Sommlending,' pipes the shrill voice of Senator Zilaris. 'If he finds the Lorestone, its power could turn the tide and save Tahou from the clutches of Darklord Gnaag.' A murmur of agreement stirs in the hall.

'And I say we should refuse to open the Cauldron,' booms the powerful voice of Senator Chil. 'I say that if it were not for his presence in our city, we would be spared the attention of the Darklords. He is the object of their anger and spite. I say we should give him to them, and in doing so we will save our city, our country, our people and ourselves!' A surge of support echoes from the arches and your skin prickles at the thought of what could happen. President Toltuda calls for a vote to decide whether the Senate should allow you to enter the Cauldron, or use you to bargain for peace with the Darklords.

Tensely you await the result. The votes are cast and counted and the Senate is split evenly: six votes for you and six votes against. The decision now rests with the President himself. He must cast the deciding vote.

Pick a number from the *Random Number Table*.

If the number you have picked is *0–4*, turn to **58**.
If the number is *5–9*, turn to **137**.

301

You are in combat with a powerful denizen of Zaaryx. There is no time to evade its attack and you must fight it to the death.

Psi-ghoul:
COMBAT SKILL 20   ENDURANCE 30

If you win the combat, turn to **87**.

302

'Never mind stranger; you are not the only one who does not know the answer,' says Khmar, motioning towards the plains farmers who are frowning and scratching their heads. He and his sons gather up their belongings and bid you goodnight. The farmers soon follow suit, leaving you and Banedon seated alone at the end of the table.

If you wish to talk to Guyuk the tavern owner, turn to **268**.
If you wish to order a meal, turn to **88**.
If you decide to call it a day and retire to your room, turn to **156**.

303

With their leader slain, the Giaks suddenly lose their nerve and fall back to their ladder. You leap forward and help them on their way with a flurry of blows that leaves six dead at your feet. Several leap from the battlements into the moat rather than stand and face your deadly counter-attack. Within minutes the wall is cleared of the enemy and a squad of Slovian mercenaries arrives to plug the gap.

If you have the Magnakai Discipline of Huntmastery and have reached the Kai rank of Principalin, turn to **35**.

If you do not possess this skill, or have yet to reach this level of Kai training, turn to **168**.

304

A tingle runs down your spine as you recognize the Chief Magistrate. It is Gwynian, the Sage of Varetta, the man who foretold the dangers of the Chasm of Doom and helped you find the Lorestone of Varetta. 'Come hither, Lone Wolf,' he beckons. His words sound in your head as if he were standing beside you, whispering them in your ear. 'Destiny has decreed that we should meet again.'

Drawn by his words and your own curiosity, you climb the steps of the Magistrates' Court and follow him to his private chambers.

Turn to **76**.

305

The man smiles smugly as you recount everything about yourself, your quest for the Lorestone, and your ordeal at the Senate House. When finally you reach the end of your account, he gives vent to a long, sardonic laugh. 'I, Maghana, the Guildmaster of Thieves, in all the years I have dwelt beneath the velvet fortress, I have dispatched many men to the Tahou Cauldron to seek out ancient treasures, though few have gone willingly and fewer still have returned alive. Know you this, Sommlending: the Cauldron is but one way to enter the main shaft to Zaaryx. There are other routes, other shafts, and all of them are known to me. I will show you one such shaft, but you must do something in return. Is it agreed?'

Cautiously you ask his terms. 'My son, Aiebek, entered the shaft three moons ago, drawn by the stories of dragon gold. He has not returned. All I ask is that if you find his body, you bring me the ring he wears upon his right hand.' Without hesitation you agree to these terms, for they seem most reasonable. He smiles, but this time his eyes glow with a strange intensity, as if he were a man on the brink of madness. 'Do not fail me,' he says, softly, holding aloft the sparkling mind-gem. 'I shall know if you lie.'

Turn to **275**.

306

The dead doomwolf drops heavily to the ground and your horse rears up on its hind legs, churning the air with its forehooves, which strike like steel hammers amid the remaining wolf-riders. More than one ends its days with your horse's hoofprint stamped upon its shattered skull. A gap appears and you see Banedon gallop past, his loose robe streaming out behind him like a pair of blue wings. You dig in your heels and urge your brave horse after him, fleeing the battleground as yet more of the wolf-riders loom into view.

Turn to **293**.

307

Suddenly you are bathed in a white light that shines upon you from holes in the stone ceiling, and at once you see the bottom of a staircase twenty yards ahead. In the corridor beyond a door swings open to reveal two reptilians, supporting on their shoulders a huge rod of crystal, encircled with tubes and with glowing metallic buttons. Terror grips your heart as you watch the rod become charged with a bolt of power that is aimed at your chest.

If you possess the Sommerswerd, turn to **27**.
If you do not possess this Special Item, turn to **152**.

308

'Your actions betray your guilt,' growls the mercenary leader. Contemptuously he hurls aside the trembling soldiers and draws his sword. 'Get 'em, lads!' he cries, and leaps to the attack.

Deldenian Mercenaries:
COMBAT SKILL 26   ENDURANCE 34

If you wish to evade after one round of combat, turn to **223**.

If you win the combat, turn to **174**.

309

You throw yourself to the ground to avoid the deadly shafts but one pierces your left arm and knocks you back several feet. You fall awkwardly, cracking your head on the hard stone floor, and opening a jagged gash above your eye: lose 8 ENDURANCE points. Blinking away the blood, which is streaming down your forehead, you grit your teeth and stagger to your feet. The sergeant yells 'Take him!' and all six of the soldiers unsheathe their weapons and run at you. You cannot evade this combat, and because the corridor is narrow, you must fight the guards two at a time.

Tower Guards 1 and 2:
COMBAT SKILL 17   ENDURANCE 29

Tower Guards 3 and 4:
COMBAT SKILL 18   ENDURANCE 32

Tower Guard and Sergeant:
COMBAT SKILL 20   ENDURANCE 32

If you win the first round of combat, Sogh will fight by your side and you may add 2 to your COMBAT SKILL for the duration of the subsequent combats.

If you win the combats, turn to **177**.

310

You steel yourself to renew your aim as the flying serpent makes its attack. At the last possible moment you release the arrow, sending it burrowing into the creature's pear-shaped skull. It gives vent to a chilling sound and somersaults backwards in the air, its wings thrashing wildly as it crashes to the ground amid a spray of blood and broken feathers.

Turn to **247**.

311

You reach the end of the alley where it joins a wide, cobblestoned avenue lit by street lanterns. A large, three-storey building stands on the corner; its windows are boarded and its doors are all locked, except for one at the side which is suspiciously ajar.

If you wish to investigate this building, turn to **217**.
If you wish to ignore it and enter the street ahead, turn to **278**.
If you decide to call off the chase, walk back to Brooker Court and continue on your way, turn to **334**.

312

A troop of guards enters the enclosure at the double. They strip you of all your Weapons, Special Items and Backpack Items, and then escort you to a cell located high in the South Gatehouse tower. Banedon is led away to another part of the city wall, to be interrogated by the gatehouse commander.

Place an 'x' beside each of the Special Items, Backpack Items and Weapons that you have listed on your *Action Chart* to indicate that they are no longer in your possession. Only if you rediscover them at a later stage of your adventure may you erase each 'x' and reuse them.

Turn to **134**.

313

The creatures possess some psychic skills that afford them a limited sixth sense. Their leader, a female, who is taller and much lighter in colour than the others, suddenly detects your presence. The sight of you frightens the creatures and they slink quickly down the stairs, cradling their egg protectively in their webbed hands. You run forward in time to see them disappear into the dark stairwell.

If you have a Kalte Firesphere, a Lantern or a Torch and Tinderbox, turn to **33**.

If you have a Fireseed and wish to throw it down the stairs, turn to **106**.

(continued over)

If you choose to unsheathe a hand weapon and
descend the stairs into darkness, turn to **224**.

314

Your suspicions are aroused as you ride towards the
watchtower. No flag flutters from its battlements and
no guards appear to challenge your approach. You
pass along a roadway littered with clothes and
belongings, and the settlement looks deserted; it is
as if the inhabitants have left in a great hurry. You
are about to spur your horse to a canter when your
Kai instincts warn you that danger lies ahead.

Like demons from a nightmare, a host of snarling
Giak wolf-riders bursts into view, streaming out from
their shadowy hiding places behind the empty huts.
They thunder towards you on every side, shrieking
and thrusting their spears at the darkening sky.

If you have a bow and wish to use it, turn to **183**.
If you wish to draw a hand weapon and prepare
for combat, turn to **244**.
If you wish to try to escape this ambush by galloping
along the pass, pick a number from the *Random
Number Table*.
If the number you have picked is *0–3*, turn to **293**.
If it is *4–9*, turn to **257**.

315

'Find somewhere else to sit, stranger: that place is
mine,' he demands, grasping the hilt of his dagger
with his free hand. You sense movement outside in
the street and you glance nervously at the cellar door.
'Get up,' growls the man impatiently, drawing his
dagger slowly from its sheath. 'If you dare cross Sogh

of Suentina, you'll not live long enough to regret it!'

At that instant the door bursts open and in rush six heavily armed Senate House guards. Thinking that the ale cellar is being raided, something of a routine event here at the Purple Purse, the shady patrons drop their drinks and flee towards the open door in an attempt to escape arrest. Sogh, the thief who threatened you, heads towards a shadowy arch. You run after him and grab him by the arm.

'Get me out of here,' you plead, 'you can name your price.' The wily thief smiles at the thought of making some easy money and holds out his hand.

'Give me your money pouch and I'll save your skin.' Grudgingly you hand over your gold and follow the thief into the archway. Delete any Gold Crowns or Lune you have recorded in the Belt Pouch section of your *Action Chart*.

Turn to **135**.

316 – *Illustration XVIII (overleaf)*

'I know where your friend is,' he says, a note of desperation creeping into his voice, 'and I know where they've stowed your equipment. Let me loose and I'll show you.' Grudgingly you undo the manacles that encircle his wrists.

'A thousand thanks,' he says, massaging his aching arms. 'My name is Sogh, master-thief of Suentina; at your service.' He bows then motions you to follow him to a closed door behind you, next to the open one through which you entered the chamber. 'This is the second time I've been invited to stay at these

XVIII.   The advancing guards drop what they are carrying
and draw their swords

lodgings,' he whispers, working on the lock with a length of wire taken from the sleeve of his leather tunic. 'Because I decided to cut short my last visit, they thought it best to keep me chained up this time.'

There is a soft click and Sogh smiles proudly as he removes the wire from the lock. 'Ha! that was easy!' he says, pushing open the door. Standing in the doorway are two burly guards, one clutching a bowl of food and the other holding a large iron key. 'Hmm . . . I thought that lock opened a bit too easily,' mumbles Sogh, as he backs away from the advancing guards. They drop what they are carrying and draw their swords; they are determined to prevent your escape.

Gatehouse Guards:
COMBAT SKILL 20   ENDURANCE 26

You must deduct 4 points from your COMBAT SKILL for the duration of the fight, as you are without a Weapon. You fight alone: Sogh is cowering behind you, using your body as a shield.

If you win the combat, turn to **259**.

317

You leap from the swinging ladder a fraction too late, overshoot the ledge, and crash painfully against a wall of rough, jagged rock. As you rebound from the wall you land on the ledge and manage to cling to the boulders that litter its surface. You have suffered cuts to your face and chest, and your side is gashed and bruised − lose 4 ENDURANCE points.

Turn to **157**.

318

Five miles along the highway you reach another junction, where a cart track bears off to the west. A whitewashed stone marker at the side of the road says:

SIDARA – 5 MILES

If you wish to follow the cart track to Sidara, turn to **45**.

If you wish to stay on the highway to Tahou, turn to **145**.

319

The soldiers demand one Crown each before even hearing your question. You pay them their price (remember to deduct this from your *Action Chart*) and ask if a blond-haired Northlander, dressed in blue robes, is being held under arrest here.

'Wait here,' says the bearded soldier, and enters the barracks. Suddenly his companion takes a swipe at you with the shaft of his halberd. Instinctively you duck, avoiding the full force of the blow, but it still catches your temple and leaves you stunned: lose 1 ENDURANCE point. 'There he is!' says the bearded man, who has reappeared with a dozen of his comrades. 'Don't let 'im get away. They want him down at the South Gate. Seems he's been givin' them a bit o' trouble.'

They surround you with a circle of spears and march you back to the South Gate tower. On the way you overhear the bearded mercenary say to another soldier, 'If only he hadn't tried to bribe us with Northland coinage, he'd have got clean away!'

Turn to **162**.

320

The lock makes an odd clicking sound but both doors remain firmly shut. Repeatedly you press the top button, running through all the numbers in the hope that it will open, but the doors do not move. You have entered part of the combination out of sequence and the lock has immobilized itself.

Turn to **207**.

321

The guards inspect the Invitation, their expressions conveying their doubt that the signature it bears is genuine. They order you to dismount and one of them hurries off to summon the gatehouse commander. Fortunately, when he arrives he recognizes Lortha's mark and allows you to leave the enclosure, although he impounds both your horses. You protest and demand that they be returned, but to no avail.

'Orders of the Senate,' says the commander, offhandedly; 'an emergency decree. All horses belonging to the civil population must be delivered into the care of the garrison stables until the state of emergency is lifted.'

Reluctantly you allow the guards to take your steeds and, as they are being led away, the commander hands you each a piece of vellum stamped with a date and a number. 'Receipts,' he explains, his tone noticeably more friendly. You pocket your Receipt (mark this as Special Item on your *Action Chart*; owing to its size, you need not delete another Special Item should you already carry the maximum quota) and are about to walk away when he calls out, 'Report to the citadel first thing in the morning. You'll be allocated your battle positions for when the enemy attack.'

Turn to **242**.

322

No sooner have you managed to prise the dead ghoul's hands from around your throat than his brethren reach the hollow. Your skin crawls at the touch of their slick, clammy flesh, but you struggle against your rising nausea and counter their attack.

Ghoul Pack: COMBAT SKILL 24   ENDURANCE 35

If you win the combat, turn to **147**.

323 — *Illustration XIX*

It is a grim grey building, devoid of decoration or colour, its stark bare walls serving to remind the Tahouese of its sober purpose. It is a place where justice is meted out to wrong-doers and harsh punishments are imposed. All trials are conducted before a magistrate and his decision is final; there are no juries in Tahou. The Chief Magistrate presides over crimes that are serious enough to warrant the death penalty and, as you stare at the courthouse from the shadows of a doorway, your pulse quickens when you see his carriage draw up outside. An old

XIX.   An old man with long grey hair and beard halts at
the top step and points his finger at you

man with long grey hair and a beard, he is wearing the purple and silver robes of the judiciary. He is accompanied by court guards and scribes, who help him to climb the steps to his private chambers located within the court building. When he reaches the top step he halts, turns, and points his finger at you.

If you have ever visited the city of Varetta or a hut on the Ruanon Pike in a previous Lone Wolf adventure, turn to **304**.

If you have never visited either of these places, turn to **263**.

324

Pressing your shoulder to the door you force it open and advance into the corridor beyond. But a shock awaits you: two reptilians kneel at the end of the passage, supporting on their scaly shoulders a huge rod of crystal encircled with tubes and glowing with metallic buttons. Terror grips your heart as you see the rod become charged with a bolt of power that is aimed at your chest.

If you possess the Sommerswerd, turn to **295**.
If you do not possess this Special Item, turn to **152**.

325

Your weapon has just cleared the scabbard when there is a tremendous noise. The snake rises into the air, its huge tree-thick body propelled by powerful feathered wings. Two vulture-like forelimbs, tipped with sharp, rending claws, scrabble at the air as it leaves its hiding place and streaks towards your chest.

Turn to **82**.

326

There is a soft whirr as the mechanism of the lock disengages, but the door does not open. *'You will need this key'* — the words sound in your head.

You spin around to see the female reptilian, the leader of her kind. She moves towards you from an archway to your right, holding a rod of Korlinium in her webbed hand. The glint of several eyes in the darkness of the other arches warn that she is not alone. Telepathically, she calls to you. *'You are unlike the other man-things that have dared to enter Zaaryx. What is it that you seek?'*

If you wish to tell her why you are here, turn to **256**.

If you choose to prepare to defend yourself in case you are attacked, turn to **83**.

327

With an outstretched hand you are able to detect the panel at the end of the passage. It is damp and crumbly and is covered with what feels like wet ropes. Suddenly one of these ropes coils around your arm, squeezing it in a vice-like grip. A wave of panic hits you as you realize you are being attacked by an angry Roctopus.

Roctopus: COMBAT SKILL 18   ENDURANCE 18

This creature is immune to Mindblast and Psi-surge. Owing to the dark and narrow confines of the passage, you must reduce your COMBAT SKILL by 4 points for the duration of the fight.

If you win the combat, turn to **139**.

328

You give a hefty kick and send a bench whirling against the man's legs. He falls heavily, slamming his head against the table and knocking himself out. The watching crowd find this greatly amusing, and while they are helpless with laughter, you escape through the door and along the street.

Turn to **146**.

329

Although you cannot gauge how deep you are, you know that your strength is fading fast. If you are to avoid a watery death, you must shed some of your equipment.

If you wish to discard half the number of items in your Backpack, turn to **91**.

If you decide to discard your Backpack completely, turn to **346**.

330

Your arrow whistles into the dark alley and seconds later you hear it shatter harmlessly against a wall. As the rapid footfalls of the Giak fade into the distance you curse his escape, for you feel sure he recognized you. When he catches up with his unit and tells them what has happened here, they are likely to return with an entire army. Wisely you decide to leave; you remount your horse and follow the track that leads out of the village.

Turn to **63**.

331

The villagers swarm around you like hungry locusts, pleading with you to buy their humble goods. Most of the baskets contain food with a greasy, off-putting smell, and small earthenware flasks full of boza — a pale yellow wine with a bouquet like sour milk. Those villagers that are too poor to offer any goods at all simply cup their hands and beg for money. For every one Gold Crown you spend here you can purchase 2 Meals or one Flask of Boza.

If you wish to give the beggars some money, turn to **163**.

If you decide to remount your horse and continue, turn to **52**.

332

Desperately you throw out your hands and manage to regain your grip of the rung. The impact has left you shaken and bruised (lose 2 ENDURANCE points) but at least you are still alive. With renewed caution you steady yourself against the jagged outcrop before continuing your descent.

Turn to **173**.

333

The commander walks slowly around your horse, his fierce gaze never once leaving your direction. 'My dear friend, your companion appears to have lost his voice,' he says to Banedon, with mock good manners. Then he signals to his men on the parapet and you hear the sound of a dozen crossbows scraping on stone as the soldiers steady their aim.

Slowly you raise your hands in surrender; to resist would be suicidal.

Turn to **312**.

334

Brooker Court ends at a plaza known as Glassblower's Square. All the shops and houses in this area are owned by the Glassblower's Guild and, as a symbol of their wealth and influence in this part of the city, each of the slabs that pave the square is made entirely of coloured glass, several feet thick. Three roads lead from this plaza of glass: Lamp Street, Southgate, and Rainbow Lane.

If you wish to go north into Lamp Street, turn to **110**.

If you choose to head south into Southgate, turn to **278**.

If you decide to go west into Rainbow Lane, turn to **245**.

335

Stones rattle beneath your horse's hooves as you skirt the slopes of the Tahou Hills. Nearly an hour slips by before you happen upon the mouth of a gorge that offers a shorter route to the north. You enter and ride along a dried-out watercourse that winds for a mile between turrets of dull-coloured rock before rising steeply into the hills. At this point a small stone hut sits overhanging the gorge. Candlelight flickers at its window and a wisp of woodsmoke rises from its chimney.

If you wish to stop and investigate the hut, turn to **18**.

If you choose to ignore it and press on, turn to **123**.

336 – *Illustration XX (overleaf)*

You raise the Sommerswerd and its golden light plays across the creature's glistening black scales. The dragon-like eyes blaze with anger and a deep growl rumbles from its cavernous mouth as it makes ready to attack.

Zadragon: COMBAT SKILL 43   ENDURANCE 58

This powerful creature is immune to Mindblast (but not Psi-surge).

If you win the combat, turn to **93**.

337

Using your Kai mastery you sense that Eastwall Lane leads directly to the Eastgate Barracks, the place where Sogh told you that Banedon is being held prisoner. Confident of your direction you ignore the other street signs and head east.

Turn to **250**.

338

Your killing blow knocks the ghoul out of the hollow, sending it tumbling into the lake. More of the corpse-like creatures can be seen creeping along the shore, and the sound of their snuffling whispers and curses makes your blood run cold. They move with unnatural speed, eager to feast on your flesh.

If you have a bow and wish to use it, turn to **22**.

(continued over)

XX.   The creature's dragon-like   eyes blaze with anger
and a deep growl rumbles from its cavernous mouth

If you wish to evade the ghouls by leaving the
   hollow and climbing the steps, turn to **104**.
If you wish to draw a hand weapon and prepare
   to fight them, turn to **254**.

339

The father and the farmers are taking it in turns to
ask each other riddles. In Anari it is forbidden to
gamble for money on games of chance, but the wily
Anarians get around the law by devious means. They
gamble on being able to answer riddles correctly,
which demands exercising skill rather than chance,
and they wager goods, and sometimes their services,
in place of money. By the time you join them the
father and his sons have amassed quite an assortment
of valuable items, and the plains farmers are clearly
anxious to win back some of their lost possessions.

If you wish to join in and take an 'Anarian gamble',
   turn to **115**.
If you do not wish to take part in their game, but
   would rather engage the tavern owner in
   conversation, turn to **268**.
If you would prefer to order a meal, turn to **88**.

340

The wagon descends a steep hill that runs parallel
to a section of the city wall under bombardment from
enemy catapults. As you near the bottom of the hill
a huge stone ball drops from the sky and slams into
the wagon, killing two horses, the captain, and you.

Tragically, your life ends here.

341

Slowly you inch your horse forward in the inky blackness until you glimpse a flickering light off to your left. You focus on this strange emanation until you can identify the source of the light. A swarm of glowing mine flies are hovering above a puddle of milky liquid, which is bubbling from a fissure in the tunnel floor. Your horse lifts its head, sniffs the cool air and gives voice to a harsh neigh of danger, for in the distant shadows something alien is stirring.

Turn to **129**.

342

The first floor is soon set ablaze as the wind whips the roof fire into a raging inferno. A soldier, his face and uniform completely blackened by soot, staggers down the stairs and collapses into your arms.

'The captain's up there . . . ' he croaks, his throat burned from inhaling the scorching air. 'He went to save his brother just before the roof caught.'

If you have the Magnakai Discipline of Nexus and
have reached the Kai rank of Principalin, turn
to **159**.

If you do not have this skill, or have yet to reach
this level of Kai training, turn to **59**.

343

The sergeant draws his curved cavalry sword and
levels it menacingly at your chest. 'By the right of
the Senate of Tahou, government of Anari,' he snarls,
in reply to your demand. 'And by the right of majority
– twenty rangers against two outlanders. Both of you
drop your weapons – at once!'

If you wish to obey the sergeant's order, turn to **24**.

If you wish to resist arrest, turn to **85**.

344

'Make sure he doesn't get away again,' commands
the officer, as his men surround you with a ring of
spears. 'This is the one that escaped from the South
Gate tower. I wouldn't like to be in his shoes when
they get their hands on him!'

The patrol march you along Rainbow Lane and then
down a street called Southgate towards the South
Gate tower. In less than fifteen minutes you find
yourself delivered back into the clutches of the angry
gatehouse guard.

Turn to **162**.

345

Using your Kai mastery, you command the deadly
Roctopus to retreat into its burrow. Slowly it responds,

drawing its slimy tentacles away from the panel as it wriggles deeper into the wall.

Turn to **139**.

346

Freed from the weight of your equipment, you are able to rise swiftly through the black water and reach the surface, coughing and gasping for air. At first the incredible coldness stunned your limbs, but now it revives your senses and spurs you towards the distant shore that gleams dimly in the faint half-light.

Aching and numb to the bone, you heave yourself out of the lake and collapse on the flat, spongy rocks that line the shore.

If you have the Magnakai Discipline of Divination, turn to **298**.
If you do not possess this skill, turn to **41**.

347

'Look out, Lone Wolf,' shouts Banedon, as you are rising from your seat. The soldier has drawn a curved dagger and he lunges forward to stab you in the heart.

If you have the Magnakai Discipline of Divination or Huntmastery, turn to **36**.
If you do not possess either of these skills, pick a number from the *Random Number Table*.
If the number you have picked is *0–6*, turn to **260**.
If it is *7–9*, turn to **119**.

348

Your companion heeds your warning and shouts a

reply, but you fail to hear what he says. A tremendous noise fills your ears as the giant snake rises into the air, lifted by a pair of powerful feathered wings. Two vulture-like legs, tipped with sharp, rending claws, scrabble the air as it dives towards your chest. A bolt of crackling energy surges past your head and streaks towards the onrushing snake. But the creature is quick to avoid Banedon's attack; it banks over to the left and the bolt arcs harmlessly into the distance. You barely have time to unsheathe a hand weapon as it closes for the kill.

Turn to **82**.

349

The reptilians hear you and fix you with frightened stares. They wrap their webbed hands around the leathery egg protectively and slink quickly down the stairs. You run to the top of the staircase and peer down into the gloom, but you can see nothing in the darkness.

If you have a Kalte Firesphere, a Lantern, or a Torch and Tinderbox, turn to **33**.

(continued over)

If you have a Fireseed and wish to throw it down the stairs, turn to **106**.

If you choose to unsheathe a hand weapon and descend the stairs into darkness, turn to **224**.

350

At the very moment of his death, the shimmering web of energy that encases the Zakhan's body flares with a scarlet brilliance so intense that you are forced to avert your eyes for fear of it blinding you. The light surges and fades, leaving behind a mound of glowing fragments that crumble and dissolve noisily until all that remains of the Zakhan and the Orb of Death is a dark stain on the earth where they fell.

Spurred on by your triumph, the Anarian defenders rally themselves and counter-attack to secure the West Gate. The Vassagonians who gained entry are either killed or forced back into the moat as the gate is quickly retaken. A cheer resounds from the city wall, a cheer that becomes a chant carrying word of Kimah's demise to the enemy beyond the moat, and gradually the advancing legions slow to a halt as their hope of an easy victory dies. Officers ride to and fro, cursing and threatening their men with all manner of punishment, but their morale is severely shaken; the ranks of armoured warriors merely stand in shocked silence and refuse to advance. The sound of distant trumpets is heard and all eyes turn to the south to see wave upon wave of mounted warriors emerging from the hills around Varta. They pour from every valley and pass to fill the southern flats with regiments of horsemen resplendent in uniforms of blue, white and grey.

'Our prayers have been answered,' says Chiban, as he and Banedon rejoin you at the city wall. 'Behold, the allies of Anari have come to aid us in our darkest hour.' He points to the advancing cavalry and you recognize, fluttering from their lances, the battle standards of three countries: Firalond, Lourden, and Kakush. Then the thunder of their horses' hooves fills the air and a wave of joy surges through you as you witness their first charge devastate the enemy's ranks, throwing them into chaos and confusion. A great battle ensues as the enemy slowly gather themselves to resist this unexpected assault. By noon two of their armies have been smashed and routed, and the third fights a desperate rearguard action as it covers the chaotic retreat westwards.

At last the fighting around the city comes to an end and the defenders give voice to their elation that their home has been saved from the hordes of Darklord Gnaag. Senator Zilaris proclaims you 'the saviour of Tahou', and the victorious cheers of the citizens echo through the burning streets and across the flats that lie stewn with enemy dead. You gaze at this grim panorama and your blood runs cold. But it is not the sight of the carnage that grips you with fear, it is your growing awareness of a powerful evil that is taking shape above the West Gate. A billowing black cloud forms in the sky, and from out of this cloud there comes a harsh and terrible voice.

'I will be avenged,' it booms, its resonance shaking the battlements on which you stand. You steel yourself, half expecting a bolt of lightning to leap from the cloud and hurtle towards you, but no such attack materializes. Instead, the chilling voice continues in a mocking tone. 'Know this; you will pay for your defiance with your life. I, Gnaag of Mozgôar, have the three remaining Lorestones that you seek, and I shall destroy them when I destroy you, Kai Lord.'

A gust of wind catches the cloud and it clears swiftly, but it leaves behind a numbing dread that fills your heart, for you sense that the words were no idle threat — the terrible voice of Darklord Gnaag spoke the truth.

Your quest has succeeded, for the wisdom and strength of the Lorestone of Tahou is now a part of your body and spirit, and your defeat of Zakhan Kimah has turned the tide of war decisively against the Darklord armies. But the shocking news that the Darklords now possess the remaining Lorestones of Nyxator heralds the start of a new and deadly perilous episode of the Magnakai quest.

If you have the courage of a true Kai Master, the

challenge of recovering the last Lorestones from the clutches of your mortal enemies awaits you, beginning in Book 10 of the Lone Wolf series, entitled:

THE DUNGEONS OF TORGAR

RANDOM NUMBER TABLE

4	0	4	8	7	4	0	9	7	5
7	6	3	6	9	6	5	6	0	2
5	8	9	3	8	0	4	7	4	5
2	7	0	4	6	8	2	5	6	4
4	8	2	4	2	3	8	2	9	5
8	2	6	8	6	7	9	8	2	8
3	0	8	4	6	1	3	5	6	9
8	0	2	7	3	5	1	7	9	4
3	8	6	5	8	1	6	8	2	6
0	8	4	6	1	0	1	6	9	5